SWEET SUMMER DAYS

SHERYL LISTER

COPYRIGHT

This book is licensed to you for your personal enjoyment only.

This is a work of fiction. Names, characters, places, and incidents are either products of the writer's imagination or are used fictitiously and are not to be construed as real. Any resemblance to actual events, locales, organizations, or persons, living or dead, is entirely coincidental.

NYLA Publishing
121 W 27th St., Suite 1201, New York, NY 10001
http://www.nyliterary.com

ACKNOWLEDGMENTS

My Heavenly Father, thank You for Your sufficient grace.

To my husband, Lance: your love, support and encouragement is what keeps me going.

Brandi, Maia, Riana, Otis, Sr., Otis Jr. and Jace, Mom (Grandma) loves you!

Thank you to my friends and family for your consistent support.

To my Club N.E.O. and Book Euphoria sisters, I love you ladies!

A huge thank you to real-life heroine Celeste Williams for supporting me from day one and allowing me to name my character after you.

To all of my readers: thank you from the bottom of my heart.

Paulette Nunlee, your editorial guidance is priceless. Thank you.

A very special thank you to my agent, Sarah E. Younger and Natanya Wheeler. I appreciate you more than I can say. You ladies are miracle workers!

DEDICATION

For Celeste Williams, a real life heroine

CHAPTER 1

"$\mathcal{I}$ brought an extra set of clothes with me tonight."

Celeste Williams nearly choked on her wine. Coughing, she set the glass down with a thud and tried to catch her breath. "Excuse me?"

"For just in case things go a little later than planned." He winked.

She stared at her dining partner and tried to wrap her mind around his obvious suggestion. She'd gone out with Clifton Brown twice, once if she didn't count the time at the coffee shop, where he had struck up a conversation while seated at the next table. "Clifton, I'm not in the habit of spending the night with a man I barely know."

"Baby, we'll know each other *real* well in a few hours."

Baby? I am too old for this. "Again, the answer is no."

Clifton's grin faded. "You're serious? I thought we were getting along pretty well."

"Very serious. You're a nice man, but maybe I'm not the woman you're looking for."

"Maybe not."

They finished their meals in strained silence, and the twenty-minute ride home felt more like two hours. She focused her attention on the passing scenery as the breeze from the warm late May temperatures blew through the partially open window. Evidently, Clifton's feelings were still hurt because once they arrived at her house, he didn't offer to walk her to the door or bother to get out of the car. In fact, he roared off before she stuck her key in the lock.

Inside, Celeste went straight to her bedroom, kicked off her shoes and sat on the side of the bed. She picked up the framed photo on her nightstand and ran her hand lovingly over the surface. Gary Williams had been gone for over four years, and she still missed him. She'd met the handsome naval officer when he had been assigned to the Defense Contract Management Agency where she worked as an industrial specialist in the production department. He'd swept her off her feet and they married nine months later. She loved everything about him, from his infectious smile to the way he could heat her up with just a look. Though Gary tended to be a little on the serious side, he never failed to keep a smile on her face. Celeste placed the photo back in its place. She'd had him for twenty-six years before cancer took him and stole their retirement dreams.

She stood and unzipped her dress. The phone rang and she groaned, then smiled upon seeing Deborah, her younger sister's name, on the display. "Hey, sis."

"Hey. Just calling to see if you're still going to go with me to Pathways tomorrow. I'm a little nervous." Pathways had opened two years ago and focused on comprehensive mental health services for veterans.

"You know I'll be there, Deb. Is TJ going?"

Deborah released a deep sigh. "No. He's convinced all they're going do is write him another prescription and said he didn't want to add addiction to his problems." Deborah's twenty-three-year-old son had been battling PTSD since his discharge eight months ago, but refused to seek treatment.

"I thought this place did more than that."

"They do. The brochure mentions support groups, outings, activities and a host of other things. But he won't budge."

Celeste felt for her nephew and couldn't imagine the horrors he'd witnessed. "What's Trent saying?"

"He thinks the center might be worth looking into, but you know men, he's not saying much else. I can tell TJ's struggles are wearing on him and every time I ask about it, he just says he's fine. The only thing he admitted to was feeling helpless because he couldn't take this away from his son."

"Well, hopefully, after we've checked it out, TJ will reconsider. What time is the support group supposed to start again? I'll be free all day."

"Yeah, yeah, whatever. Not everybody can retire at fifty-three."

She laughed. "Don't hate. I gave the federal government thirty years and that was enough. These last six months have been glorious." When her department had reorganized and downsized, she'd qualified for early retirement due to her service time and decided to take it. The payments she received from Gary's military and private sector jobs had afforded her options that many people didn't have.

"The one for family members starts at two, but I plan to leave work around noon. How about I pick you up and we go have lunch first?"

"Sounds good to me."

"Speaking of food, how did your date with Clifton go?"

Celeste blew out a weary breath. "Girl, don't ask."

Deborah chuckled. "That bad?"

"Worse. Over dinner he told me that he'd packed an extra set of clothes in case things ran longer tonight."

She burst out laughing. "Are you *serious*?"

"I was so outdone, I almost choked on my wine."

"You gotta give the brother credit. He's a planner," Deborah said.

"Whatever. Is this what dating looks like now? Never mind. I don't know why I'm asking you." Deborah had been married to Trent, Sr. for twenty-five years and her brother-in-law loved his wife to distraction.

"Sorry, sis. I don't believe all men are like Clifton. There are some good ones available."

"Yeah, well, I think I should just forget this whole dating thing. Back when Gary and I dated, rarely would a man be so presumptuous after a second date to suggest spending the night." Memories of the times she and Gary spent taking long walks in the park and talking for hours surfaced in her mind. Her heart clenched.

"Maybe that's the problem, Celeste. You're looking for someone exactly like Gary. I agree that he might be a tough act to follow, but you can't expect every man you meet to be Gary's reincarnation."

"I know that, and maybe I am subconsciously doing as you said, but I want a man who treats me like he did." Celeste wanted someone to open her doors, talk to her about nothing and everything and to snuggle with while they watched movies and stuffed their faces with popcorn and root beer floats.

"There are men who do that. Honey, are you sure you're ready to move on?"

For a moment, she didn't reply. Was she ready? Admittedly, loneliness reared its ugly head more often than not, and perhaps she'd been using the dating as a coping mechanism. In reality, that had been the only reason she'd gone out with Clifton. Prior to that, she hadn't been on a date in eight months. Her twenty-nine-year-old son, Emery, made a point of calling or visiting at least twice a week. Celeste appreciated his efforts, but she wanted him to live his own life. "I honestly don't know. It's not like I'm sitting here pining away for Gary. He's not coming back.

I've been enjoying life, traveling and doing some of the things we always said we'd do, but I just wish... Oh, I don't know." She'd traveled to D.C. to visit the National Museum of African American History and gone on a cruise to the Caribbean.

"You just wish you had someone there to love you and do all the things that come with being in a relationship."

"Sometimes. And other times I feel guilty."

"You have nothing to feel guilty about. As you said, Gary isn't coming back. You two had a wonderful marriage, but you're a beautiful woman with a lot of life left. If it's meant to be, you'll find someone who will do all those things with you. He'll do them *his* way and you two can create some new and wonderful memories."

"You know, I'm the older sister. I should be the one giving out all this good advice," Celeste said wryly.

"You're welcome."

"Love you, Deb."

"I love you, too. Now, I need to go to bed because, unlike someone else who shall remain nameless, I have to go to work on a Tuesday morning."

She laughed softly. "You'll get there. I'll see you tomorrow."

"Good night, big sis."

"Night." Celeste sat holding the phone. She did have more life in her. However, rather than navigating the waters of dating again, she began to think she should just take her memories and be happy.

"Look who's back." Thaddeus Whitcomb opened the door wider to let his best friends, Nolan Gray and his wife, DeAnna in. He patted Nolan on the shoulder. "You look ten years younger since retirement. Hey, Dee." He kissed her cheek. "Come on back. You guys want something?" He and Nolan shared a friendship that spanned nearly forty years and began when the two eighteen-year-olds met in the Army.

They followed him to the family room and sat on the sofa. Nolan said, "We're fine."

Thad reclaimed his favorite recliner. "So how was Hawaii?"

"Heavenly," DeAnna said. "If I had known how much fun we'd be having, I would've told him to retire years ago."

Nolan shook his head. "Woman, you act like we never went anywhere before now."

"Rarely," she teased. "You and Thad had to be pried out of those offices."

Thad laughed. "She does have a point." After their discharge from the Army—he, for medical reasons and Nolan, after finishing his tour of duty— they had been disheartened by the difficulty in getting services and accommodations for the disabled. Nolan decided to design them himself and started Gray Home Safety. Thad joined the company as a partner soon after. He and Nolan had a long-standing agreement that the company would remain in their families, with a Gray as CEO and a Whitcomb as vice president. They'd retired two years ago and Nolan's oldest son, Brandon, and Thad's daughter, Faith, who'd married shortly afterwards, now held those roles.

"Man, how're you going to take her side?"

"Nolan, you and I may go way back, but I'm not getting on Dee's bad side." He and Nolan laughed. "She's sweet, but she's also direct and doesn't mince words."

DeAnna stared on with mock offense. "Really, you two?"

Nolan leaned over and gave his wife a quick kiss. "You know I love you, baby."

"Mmm hmm." She waved him off. "Anyway, Thad, you should take a trip to Hawaii soon."

"I may have to do that." He had only taken two short trips in the last two years, one to San Diego and the other to San Francisco. Both alone.

"I'm sure any number of women would love to take the trip with you. It's so romantic."

"Uh oh," Nolan said. "She's on her matchmaking campaign again."

DeAnna playfully swatted Nolan on the arm. "Oh, hush. Don't you think it's about time for Thad to find someone?"

He held up his hands. "I'm staying out of this. Thad, I love you like a brother, but you're on your own."

Thad smiled. "Some friend you are." He'd dated in the thirty years since his divorce, and though he had come close once, he hadn't found that one special woman yet.

DeAnna continued as if the two men hadn't spoken. "Rose asked about you again."

His smile faded. He had met Rose at their youngest son, Malcolm's wedding a few of months ago. She had made her interest clear and, although she seemed like a nice lady, he hadn't felt any attraction toward her. "Come on, Dee. I already told you I'm not interested in Rose. I told her the same thing at the wedding reception, so I don't understand why she's still asking about me."

"Probably that dance," she said with a chuckle. "She couldn't stop talking about your nice smile, dark good looks and toned body. She asked me how you kept in such good shape at your age, but I figured you didn't want me telling all your secrets, so I told her she should ask you."

He lifted a brow. "At my age? I'm only fifty-five. Exactly how old did you tell her I was?"

Nolan doubled over laughing.

DeAnna shrugged. "I just told her we were around the same age."

Thad shook his head. "Dee, she'd better not show up at the gym." Thad had a membership at the gym owned by Nolan and Dee's second oldest son, Khalil. "I know how you are," he added with a laugh. She'd been trying to match him with one woman after another over the years.

"I don't know what you mean."

"Baby, that innocent act won't work. Thad has known you way too long. If he needs some help finding that perfect woman, he'll ask."

Thad slanted Nolan an incredulous look. "No I won't." He'd had no problems in the dating area...when he chose to date. True, he sometimes missed the companionship that came with being in a relationship, but he had no plans to settle down with any woman who came along just because the loneliness started talking. He glanced down at his watch. "I need to head over to the center." Thad volunteered at Pathways, a comprehensive mental health center founded by Omar Drummond, the LA Cobras football team's star receiver and his friends' son-in-law.

"Are you leading a group today?" Nolan asked.

"No. I told Phillip I'd sit in on his family support group." He knew all too well the impact PTSD had on the family. Had it not been for his two friends and some good counseling, he didn't know where he'd be.

They stood and DeAnna said, "Tell Omar we'll be by to see the new basketball court soon."

Thad walked them to the door. "I will. If I don't talk to you before, I'll see you two on Saturday." Faith and Brandon were expecting their first child and, unlike typical baby showers, the Grays tended to make it a family event. They said their good-byes, and Thad left for the center.

When he arrived, he met Omar coming down the hall.

"Hey, Unc," Omar said, pulling Thad into a one-armed hug. Nolan's children had adopted him as an uncle and when Omar married into the family, he'd taken to calling Thad the same.

"Hey, Omar. How's school?"

"The semester is almost over, thank goodness." He was enrolled in a psychology PhD program.

"Morgan and the baby doing okay?" Morgan, along with her twin brother, Malcolm, were the youngest of the Gray clan.

"They're good, but since Little Omar started walking a couple of weeks ago, the boy is all over the place. I didn't know a ten-month-old could get into so much stuff and so fast. Last night, he pushed something on my laptop and the screen went blank. I was typing my paper and almost had a heart attack."

Thad laughed. "Were you able to recover your information?"

"After about thirty minutes of sweating and trying everything known to man, including calling a tech person. Thankfully, I'd just saved the file, so I didn't lose anything."

A memory surfaced of Faith at that age and he smiled, then his heart clenched. He'd lost her a year later and spent the next twenty-eight years trying to find her.

Someone called out to Omar and he turned. "Be right there." To Thad he said, "I'll see you later."

Thad threw up a wave to the counselor who'd flagged Omar, then continued down the hall and around the corner. His steps slowed when he spotted a woman slumped against the wall, arms wrapped around her middle, with tears streaming down her face. Concerned, he hurried to where she stood. "Is everything okay?"

She seemed to just notice him and hastily wiped at the tears. "Oh, yes. I'm fine." She tried to smile.

"Are you sure? How about we sit at one of these tables over here and I get you some water?" He pointed to the dining hall a few feet from where they stood. He gently guided her into the room and seated her before bringing a box of tissues and some water. Their hands touched during the exchange and he felt a spark of awareness.

She accepted the items, pulled a few tissues out and blotted at the tears. "Thank you."

This time when she smiled at him, Thad felt a strange sensation. One he hadn't experienced in quite a while—immediate attraction. "I'm Thad."

"Celeste. Do you work here?"

"No. I volunteer a few hours a week. Are you attending one of the groups?"

She nodded.

"Your husband?"

"No. I came with my sister. Her son is struggling with PTSD and she's pretty much at the end of her rope."

Thad took a quick glance at her left hand and didn't see a wedding ring, but that didn't mean anything. Surprised, he wondered why he even cared. His gaze went back to her face. Her tear-stained dark brown eyes were set in a gorgeous golden face. She took a sip of the water and her tongue darted out to capture a drop on the corner of her mouth. Arousal hummed in his veins. "I'll be right back. I need to tell Phillip where I am."

She nodded.

What is going on? I'm too old for this kind of thing. Or was he?

CHAPTER 2

*C*eleste placed the bottle of water on the table and fanned herself. Her heart raced and she didn't know which had affected her more—the support group or the caring man who'd brought her tissues and water. *Goodness, that man is fine!* He had to be at least six feet tall and stood with perfect posture. By the way he carried himself, she put him close to her age. She chastised herself for the wayward thought. Her focus needed to be solely on helping her family. She jumped slightly when Thad's hand brushed her shoulder as he reclaimed his seat.

"I'm sorry. I didn't mean to startle you."

His deep, soothing voice floated over her like a warm embrace. *Okay, girl. Get it together. You're acting like a teenager.* "I was sitting here thinking, that's all."

"You said you were here with your sister. Did something happen in the group?"

"No. Listening to the shared stories just got to be a little overwhelming. Outside of the issues with my nephew, I never knew how hard this disease is on families." The story about a young man so traumatized by what he'd seen that he would crawl under his bed and not come out for days had been the one that broke Celeste. She'd barely held it together long enough to leave the room. "Trent—my nephew—has been back eight months. My sister says he has nightmares and she sometimes finds him prowling the house at night. He told her if he didn't sleep, he'd have no nightmares."

Thad nodded. "It's tough, and that's why Omar founded this center. We want to do everything we can to help these men and women transition back to civilian life and regain some level of wholeness."

She studied him. "You sound like you know a lot about it."

A slight smile curved his mouth. "More than I care to know. I volunteer here because I've been where they are."

"You're a veteran?"

"Yes, ma'am."

Celeste reached over and squeezed his hand. "Thank you so much for your service."

Thad placed his other hand over hers. "It was my honor."

For a moment, neither of them moved. She realized their hands were still connected and quickly, but gently, pulled away. She jumped up from the chair. "I…um…I should get back in there. My sister is probably wondering where I am."

He stood. "Come on. I'll go with you."

"Oh, you don't have to do that. Didn't you mention you were volunteering?"

He smiled. "This is part of what I do, Celeste."

The way he said her name sounded like a sweet caress. Celeste shook herself. "Okay. Thank you." They entered the room quietly and she sat next to her sister. Thad grabbed a chair and sat behind her.

Deborah divided a glance between Celeste and Thad, and then mouthed, "I want all the details."

Celeste turned her attention to the person speaking. A few more people shared their stories and she nudged Deborah, but Deborah shook her head.

"Maybe next time," she whispered.

The man facilitating the group, who had introduced himself as Phillip, waited until everyone who'd wanted to share had done so. "I want to thank you all for coming today. A good support system is the first step in helping your loved one. The more you learn about PTSD, the better you'll be equipped to handle it. Consider planning dinner out, going to a movie, taking a walk or bike ride, or some other activity. Exercise is important for your health and does wonders for clearing the mind. But also understand your family member may not want to talk and could possibly withdraw. Recognize that these can be symptoms of PTSD. Give them the space they need, but remind them you'll be there whenever they're ready." Phillip glanced around the room. "Does anyone have anything else they'd like to say or have any questions?" He waited a moment. When no one said anything, he said, "I see a few new faces this week and I hope you'll come back. There are some brochures on the back table with more information about the programs here and how to contact us. Thanks for coming. I'll be around if anyone wants to talk."

People made their way to the table. Before Celeste could suggest to Deborah that they do the same, Thad came over and handed them both a stack of papers.

"Thank you." Deborah stuck out her hand. "I'm Deborah Chapman."

Thad shook her hand. "Thad Whitcomb."

"It's nice to meet you. Is this your first time, too?"

He smiled. "Nice meeting you, too. And no. I've been around since before they broke ground. I volunteer here a few hours a week."

"That's wonderful." Deborah slanted a quick glance at Celeste. "Don't you think so, sis?"

Celeste stifled an eye-roll. She knew exactly how Deb operated. "Yes, I do. Didn't you say you wanted to beat the traffic?"

The drive from Hawthorne to Long Beach should take less than half an hour, but she could count the number of times there'd been no traffic on the 405 on one hand and still have fingers left.

Deborah didn't answer, but her amusement was plain.

Thad retrieved two cards from his wallet and handed them to Celeste and Deborah. "If either of you needs to talk, please don't hesitate to contact me or Phillip."

She accepted the card. "Thank you. That's very nice of you."

"Will your husbands be joining you for the next session?"

Celeste opened her mouth to answer and Deborah jumped in. "I'm going to try to get my husband to come. Celeste isn't married."

She wanted to pop her sister.

"Celeste, would you give me a call tomorrow so I know you're okay?" Thad asked.

Celeste hesitated briefly. "Sure."

"I'll let you ladies get going. It was nice meeting you and I hope to see you again."

He'd said the words to both of them, but his eyes remained on Celeste and she could sense the attraction rising between them. "Thanks again for everything, Thad." She and Deborah made their way out to the car and Celeste said, "I don't want to hear it."

"Hear what?" Deborah asked with a laugh. "You don't want to hear about all the heat you and Mr. Fine-as-wine Thad Whitcomb were generating." She turned in her seat. "How did you happen upon him?"

"He saw me in the hallway crying when I stepped out of the session and sat with me in the dining hall for a few minutes."

She pulled out onto the road. "He seems nice."

Celeste stared out the window. "Yeah, he does." She still felt baffled by her reaction to him. She hadn't experienced that kind of sensation since…Gary. Guilt rose, but she pushed it down.

"I think he's interested in you. And you know what else?"

She was afraid to ask. "What?"

"You're interested in him, too." Deborah held up a hand. "And before you try to lie, I saw the way you looked at him."

She whipped her head around. "What way is that?"

"Your eyes were glued to him when he walked over after the meeting."

"I don't know what you're talking about?" Had she really been staring at him?

"I can't blame you, though, because the brother looks *good*. Hmm, I wonder how old he is. Well, you can find out all that information when you call him tomorrow."

"I'm only calling him to let him know I'm okay. Which I am. Nothing more."

"Whatever you say, big sis. But I say, if he asks you out, you should say yes. Any man who shows concern toward a woman he doesn't know can't be all bad. Hey, he can't be worse than Clifton."

Celeste groaned. "Please don't mention that man."

Deborah shrugged. "Might as well have a good dinner date to erase the memories of a bad one."

"You're acting like Thad has already asked me out. He hasn't and most likely won't. He's just concerned. Remember, this is part of what he does at the center." Wanting to change the subject, she asked, "So what did you think of the group?"

Deborah sobered. "I liked it. It felt good to know we aren't the only ones going through this. I mean, I already knew that, but being in the room and actually *hearing* some of the same things Trent and I have been experiencing with TJ helped a lot. I also like that they're focused on complete wellness—mind, body and soul—and not just handing out prescriptions."

"I hear you. That's what stuck with me, too."

"I'm going to talk to Trent about coming next week. He needs to hear how other fathers are coping. I don't think TJ will, but I'm going to try some of the suggestions Phillip gave about going out to dinner. TJ's favorite restaurant is Harold and Belle's and we haven't even gone since he's been home."

"I love that place, too." Just thinking about the Creole menu made her mouth water.

"You should come with us. I figure going during the week might be better, so we can avoid the weekend crowd. I'm not sure how he'll do with that."

"Let me know when."

"Now, back to Thad."

Celeste sighed. Four years her junior, Deborah had always had laser-like focus and, no matter how they tried, Celeste and her parents could never steer her away from a topic for too long. Deborah would go along with their tactics for a few minutes, then circle back around to what she wanted.

"There is no back to Thad. Like I said, he's just being nice."

"And like *I said*, he's interested. Can you do me a favor?"

"What is it?"

"If he asks you out, say yes. Even if it turns out to be nothing, you deserve to spend time with a nice man, and Thad seems very nice."

Celeste couldn't argue that point. "I'll think about it." She figured she'd call tomorrow, as promised, and that would be the extent of it. Their paths might cross at the center, if she chose to accompany Deb again, but she didn't see it going any further. Besides, a man like Thad most likely wasn't single.

WEDNESDAY MORNING, THAD SAT IN THE GRAY HOME SAFETY board meeting listening to Brandon give updates on all the new projects. All of the Gray children had seats on the board, but only Brandon and Siobhan, the oldest and who served as PR director, worked for the company. Of particular interest to Thad was the additional equipment Khalil had designed for his fitness centers. He'd transformed a section of the gym to accommodate those who were in wheelchairs, had limbs amputated or other disabilities, added free weights with Braille and installed a section of flooring that had the same feel as a mat, but without the uneven surface for those with low vision or blindness.

When the meeting ended, he spent a few minutes talking with Nolan and Brandon, then made his way to the exit.

Khalil stopped him at the door. "Hey, Unc. I have a new stationary bike I want you to try out. I made some adjustments to the pedal to help keep the feet in place."

"I'll be by as soon as I can." Thad had lost his lower left leg in Desert Storm and his prosthesis tended to slide off the normal pedal.

He laughed. "Gotta keep in shape for the ladies, huh? Don't think I haven't noticed a few of them checking you out."

Thad waved him off. Celeste was the only woman who held his interest at the moment. "Just trying to keep this old body from getting too *old*."

"You aren't old, just experienced."

He chuckled. "Yeah, experienced." He clapped Khalil on the shoulder. "I want to talk to Faith before I leave."

"Okay. I'll see you on Saturday."

Still smiling, Thad left the conference room and went to Faith's office. He knocked on the partially open door.

"Come in."

Thad entered and watched her fingers fly over the keyboard.

A moment later, Faith glanced his way. "Dad." She stood and rushed around the desk as fast as her eight-month pregnant body allowed.

He engulfed her in a strong hug. He still couldn't believe she was back in his life after twenty-eight years of searching, and that made his world perfect. "How're you feeling?"

"Not too bad. Brandon is making me cut my hours here

because my feet have been swelling. I don't really mind because I can run my website business with my feet up."

Thad smiled. "Has he decided who's going to fill in for you here while you're on maternity leave?"

She waved a hand. "You know Brandon. He said he didn't need anyone."

"That boy is never going to change." Brandon had always expected to run the company solo because no one outside of Nolan and Dee knew that Thad had a daughter. Unbeknownst to Brandon, the woman he'd assisted in a car accident and begun dating, turned out to be his second-in-command. Thad recalled all the fireworks that announcement had caused. In the end, everything had worked out well. He opened his mouth to say something and his cell rang. He pulled out the phone and checked the display, but didn't recognize the number and debated whether to answer.

"Aren't you going to answer that?" Faith asked.

Thad connected. "Hello?"

"Hello, Thad. It's Celeste."

The sound of her voice made his smile widen. "Celeste, how are you?"

"I'm fine. As I mentioned yesterday, it was just a little over-whelming hearing the stories for the first time."

"I'm glad to hear it. And your sister?"

"She's hopeful."

"Good. Do you plan to be at next week's session with her?"

"I don't know."

Thad wanted to see her again, but didn't want to chance a missed opportunity if she didn't come to the meeting. He hesi-tated briefly. "Would you like to have lunch on Friday, if you're not busy? I can meet you somewhere near your job or we can wait until the weekend."

Celeste's soft laughter came through the line. "I retired a few months ago, and Friday will be fine."

He frowned. She didn't look old enough to be retired. "Great. I'll need your address, so I can pick you up." He turned and Faith, with a big grin on her face, handed him a pad and pen. He tried to hide his own as he wrote down Celeste's information. They said their goodbyes and he disconnected.

"Well, now. Looks like somebody's got a new lady. You should bring her to the baby shower."

"I don't have a new lady. I just met her yesterday at the center." Thad shared the details of the encounter.

"I'm glad you were there. Does she have potential?"

"Maybe. She seems nice." His reaction to her made him speculate on whether she had more than potential.

Faith placed her hand on his arm. "You deserve someone special, Dad. Especially, after everything."

They fell silent, both remembering the lost years. Not wanting the past to rise up and consume him, he said, "I'd better let you get back to work. Do you guys need me to do anything for the shower?"

"I don't think so, but Brandon or I will let you know." She came up on tiptoe, kissed his cheek and hugged him.

"Take care of yourself and my grandbaby."

"I will. You missed out on raising me, but I'm so glad you'll be around to spoil this one." Faith placed a hand on her rounded belly.

"So am I, baby girl." Emotion clogged his throat. He kissed her forehead. "Love you, sweetheart, and don't overdo it."

She let out a short bark of laughter. "As if my husband would allow it." They shared a smile. "I'll see you later. Oh, and keep me posted on Ms. Potential."

"Yeah, okay." Laughing, Thad exited. It had been a while since he'd been so excited about a date and he was looking forward to seeing Celeste.

CHAPTER 3

*C*eleste entered Harold and Belle's restaurant Thursday evening and searched the area for her sister and family. She spotted them on the far side of the room and indicated that to the hostess before starting in their direction.

Her brother-in-law rose to his feet and kissed her cheek. "Hey, Celeste."

"Hi, Trent. I like the beard." His normally clean-shaven face now sported a neatly barbered low dusting of hair. "Hey, TJ." She shifted to hug her nephew and felt her emotions rise. The outgoing young man she'd watched grow up had been transformed by war to a stoic one. TJ rarely smiled now, he'd lost weight and, in his eyes, she noted a weariness typically reserved for someone much older.

"How are you Auntie?"

She and Deborah shared a quick hug and Celeste sat before answering. "I'm good. How are you doing?"

TJ shrugged. "Today, not so bad."

A server passed with a tray of food and the smell wafted into her nose and made her mouth water. She smiled. "And it'll get better once we eat all this delicious food."

A slight smile tilted the corner of his mouth.

Deborah mouthed a silent thank you to Celeste and picked up her menu. "We were waiting for you before ordering."

Celeste pored over the menu and couldn't decide between the fried catfish and jambalaya.

Deborah suggested she order one of the combination plates that featured both. "You can always have the leftovers for lunch tomorrow."

She opened her mouth to tell her sister she wouldn't need lunch tomorrow because she had a date, but immediately changed her mind. "True." She would just wait to see how it went before saying anything. After ordering, conversation flowed around the table. They all tried to draw TJ in, but he made few comments. When the food arrived, Celeste went for the catfish. The fish was crisp on the outside, tender on the inside and almost melted in her mouth. "How's the gumbo, TJ?"

His mouth curved into the first real smile she had seen in a long while. "Better than I remember."

"Better than mine?" Deborah asked with a raised eyebrow.

TJ leaned over and kissed her cheek. "Nobody's gumbo is better than yours, Mom."

Trent shook his head. "Son, now you know she's going to be bragging for the next two weeks."

"You've got that right." She patted TJ's hand. "And I'll make you some this weekend, just so you can be sure."

Celeste laughed. "Girl, you are a mess."

"Mmm hmm, but you know you want me to save you some." Deborah sipped her tea.

She couldn't deny it. They had both learned to cook from their mother and their grandmother, who lived in Louisiana. However, Deborah knew her way around the kitchen almost as well as the southern matriarch. Everyone laughed, then finished their meals while keeping up a steady stream of conversation.

When it came time to leave, Deborah stood. "Let me hit this bathroom before we go."

Celeste followed suit. "I should probably do the same." She had consumed two glasses of tea.

"I'll take care of the bill and we'll meet you by the front door. And Celeste, don't bother pulling out your money."

She had known Trent would say that. "Okay, but I'm leaving the tip." Before he could argue, she placed a bill on the table and followed her sister to the bathroom.

On the way back, Deborah asked, "Did you call Thad yesterday?"

"Yes, and I told him I was fine."

"That's it? No conversation, plans to talk again…*nothing?*"

Celeste angled her head toward Deborah. "He asked me out to lunch."

Deborah pumped her fist in the air. "Alright! Now, we're getting somewhere."

The two women reached the front where Trent and TJ stood waiting. "We haven't gotten anywhere, Deb. It's lunch."

"And if it becomes dinner and more?"

"I have no idea." Celeste didn't want to think beyond tomorrow. She hugged her brother-in-law and nephew. "Thanks for inviting me to dinner." She reached for Deborah.

"I'll call you tomorrow for all the details," Deborah whispered.

She chuckled. "Can you at least wait until the lunch hour ends?"

Deborah gave her a sidelong glance. "Whatever, girl."

They parted ways in the parking lot and Celeste drove home. Her cell rang as soon as she closed the door. She figured Deb wanted to make sure she had gotten home safely, as usual. She dug her cell out and answered without looking at the display. "Yes, sis. I'm home, safe and sound."

"I'm glad to hear it," said the warm baritone.

Her pulse skipped. She snatched the phone away and stared at the screen. She placed it back on her ear. "Hi, Thad."

"Did I catch you at a bad time?"

"Oh, no. Um...I just got home from dinner with my sister's family. We try to get together regularly." Celeste shook her head. She stood in the middle of her living room stammering like a sixteen-year-old. She took a deep breath. "Is something wrong? Do we need to cancel lunch?"

Thad laughed softly. "There's nothing wrong, Celeste."

Something about the way he said her name always set the butterflies to dancing in her belly.

"I only wanted to hear your voice and let you know how much I'm looking forward to seeing you tomorrow."

Oh, my! Celeste's hand came up to her rapidly beating heart. "So am I."

"Well, I won't hold you. I'll pick you up at twelve-thirty. Good night and sleep well."

"Good night." She held the phone against her chest and closed her eyes. For the first time in four years, she felt herself responding to a man.

FRIDAY, THAD CHECKED THE REARVIEW MIRROR ONCE MORE. HE'D gone to get a haircut earlier and had taken extra care when shaving that morning. He got out, retrieved the vase containing an arrangement of pink roses and headed up the walk. Celeste opened the door a few seconds after he rang the bell. Thad hadn't imagined her beauty. Today, she wore a sleeveless black and white dress and a pair of black low-heeled sandals, giving him a perfect view of her toned arms and legs. Her short, layered hair didn't have a strand out of place and the bronze color on her full lips made him want to find out if they were as lush as they appeared. He finally found his voice. "You look stunning. These are for you," he said, handing her the vase.

Celeste's eyes lit up. "They're gorgeous, thank you. Come in." She stepped back for him to enter.

Thad followed and watched the sweet sway of her hips. The beige and brown décor reminded him of his own place. She placed the vase on a coffee table. "I should have asked if you had a restaurant preference. My apologies."

She smiled. "No apologies needed. I'm sure whatever restaurant you chose will be fine."

"I made reservations at Parkers' Lighthouse in Shoreline Village, if that's okay."

"More than okay. I've heard of it, but have never been." She picked up her purse. "I'm ready if you are."

"More than ready," he said, echoing her words. Their eyes held for a long moment, then he led her out to his car. Thad held the door open for Celeste, then closed it behind her and got in on the driver's side.

"Buicks have come a long way. This is far more stylish than the older models."

Thad chuckled and started the engine. "Yes, they have. I bought it about four years ago and it still rides well." As they drove off, he turned the air down. "Let me know if the temperature is too cold or hot."

"This is good. I see you like Brian Culbertson."

Thad slanted her a quick glance. "He's a talented young man. I saw him in concert a few years ago and have been buying his music ever since."

"I know what you mean. He puts on a phenomenal show."

"Who else do you listen to?"

Celeste shifted in her seat to face him. "I love Boney James, Kirk Whalum, Maysa, Lalah Hathaway and, honey, give me everything Will Downing."

He laughed, enjoying the excitement in her voice. They continued talking about music, movies and some of their favorite places to visit, and he found that they had a lot in common. By the time they reached the restaurant located at the tip of Shoreline Village, Thad had already decided to ask her out again. He parked, helped her out of the car and escorted her into the restaurant. A hostess led them to a table outside on the patio that offered a panoramic view of the Queen Mary and Long Beach Harbor. The near eighty-degree temperatures made it the perfect spot. Thad seated Celeste and the soft notes of her perfume drifted to his nose. It smelled sweet and suited her perfectly.

"This is very nice, Thad. Thank you."

"Thank you for agreeing to lunch." She gave him a shy smile and his heart thumped in his chest. A server brought glasses of water and took their drink order. For the next few minutes he and Celeste searched the menu.

"I see so many things I'd like to try."

"Feel free to try as many as you like."

Her head came up and she stared at him with a strange look on her face. "I beg your pardon?"

Thad repeated his statement. "And whatever you don't eat, you can have for leftovers. Just think of it as taking a night off from cooking."

Celeste lowered the menu. "That's a generous offer, but one entrée is more than enough. Besides, I have food from last night's dinner at Harold and Belle's with my family."

He leaned back in the chair. "Man, I haven't been there in a while."

"Maybe we can go—" She cut herself off, as if realizing what she'd said.

Thad reached for her hand. "I'm counting on it." Smiling, he went back to his menu. After the server left drinks and took their order, the conversation continued with a relaxed camaraderie reserved for old friends. They shared a lobster and shrimp taquitos appetizer. Celeste ordered the crab cake sandwich with french fries and he had the Tuscan chicken sandwich with cole slaw. Over the meal, Thad asked the question that had been bugging him since their phone conversation two days ago. "You mentioned that you're retired. Please don't take offense, but you don't look anywhere near old enough for retirement."

She laughed. "No offense taken at all. I appreciate the compliment. I worked for the federal government for thirty years, and when they reorganized, I took advantage of the early retirement option a few months ago. It was my Christmas present to me."

"That's the best kind of gift."

Celeste took a sip of her lemonade. "I know you volunteer at the mental health center, but what else do you do?"

Thad leaned back in his chair. "Like you, I've been enjoying the retired life for two years."

"*Two years?*" She scrutinized him for a long moment. "I can say the same thing about you—you don't look anywhere near retirement age."

He grinned and lifted his glass. "You know what they say about good Black."

She touched her glass to his. "Amen." They went back to their meals.

He and Celeste were still laughing and talking when they left the restaurant. He reached for her hand and threaded their fingers together. He sensed the same awareness he'd felt at the center. He waited for her to pull away and was pleased that she didn't. Celeste glanced down at their hands, then back up at him and smiled. "Would you like to walk around for a while?"

"I'd love to. It's such a nice day and I need to walk off a few of those french fries."

Thad's gazed roamed down her slender curves. "You're a

beautiful woman, Celeste, and I don't see anything that needs to be walked off. I like everything just where it is."

Celeste let out a little chuckle. "Um...okay. If you say so."

"I absolutely do." A rush of color flooded her cheeks. He just smiled and started up the block. Yes, he was beginning to like this woman.

CHAPTER 4

Several colorfully painted shops lined the boardwalk and people stopped here and there taking photographs. Celeste hadn't said a word since his statement. Unlike the last few men she had gone out with whose compliments were better suited for a twenty-something at a club, Thad's words let her know that he didn't fall into that category. The warmth of his strong hand holding hers and the ease at which they conversed had her somewhat off balance. She had spent the last few years celibate by choice and it hadn't bothered her once. Today, however, her body reminded her that she was, in fact, still a woman with needs.

"You were right about this being a beautiful day. If you want to stop in any of the shops, just let me know."

"I'm just enjoying walking and looking at the water." In actuality, Celeste felt a contentment that scared her. At length, they reached Ice Cream on the Boardwalk and his steps slowed.

"Since we didn't have dessert, how about some ice cream?"

"I'd love some." She really should have declined after having an appetizer and her meal, but one scoop of her favorite strawberry ice cream wouldn't hurt. He purchased them both cones and they sat at one of the tables to eat.

"This is good," Thad said, taking another lick.

The sight of his tongue making a long stroke around the creamy confection sent a shock of desire straight to her core. Celeste tore her gaze away and focused on the water. She tried to get the image out of her head, but it wouldn't leave. All she could think about was how it would feel to have his tongue stroking her the same way. She must be losing her mind sitting here contemplating such crazy ideas with a man she'd just met. Even though she and Gary had a short engagement, she didn't recall having all these immediate physical reactions to him. "I agree." Celeste started in on her own cone, hoping it would cool her off.

"Do you have any other plans for the weekend?"

"If you call cleaning and laundry having plans, then, yes, I have plenty," she said with a little laugh. "What about you?"

"Going to a baby shower for my daughter. Her husband's family typically does showers that involve the whole clan."

"Wow, so one big party."

"Pretty much."

"Do you have any other children?"

"No, just the one." A shadow crossed his face. "What about you?"

"I have one son." Celeste studied him for a moment, wondering about the split second of sadness. Did he and his daughter have problems? She opened her mouth to ask another question and her cell rang in her purse. Knowing it was most likely Deborah wanting an update, she let it go to voicemail. It rang again and she sighed.

Thad chuckled. "You might want to answer that. It seems like someone really wants to talk to you."

She smiled. "Probably my sister being nosy." She dug it out, saw her son, Emery's name on the display and connected.

"Mom, I've been calling the house for the past couple of hours and sent you two texts. Where are you?" Emery said before she could get a word in.

"Hello to you, too, Emery."

"Sorry," he mumbled. "Hi. I was just worried."

"Why? This isn't the first time I've left the house for more than a few hours, son. I'm out right now and I'll call you later."

"Out with who?"

Celeste lifted a brow. "You do remember that I'm the mother? I'll talk to you later," she said in a tone that brokered no argument.

"Okay."

She disconnected, dropped the phone back in her purse and shook her head. "Good grief."

Thad shifted to face her. "Is he okay?"

"Oh, he's fine. Ever since his father died, he acts like I can't leave the house without getting his permission."

He draped his arm around her shoulders. "I'm sorry. How long has it been?"

"A little over four years."

"Sounds like you loved him very much."

"I did." Not wanting to dwell on the memories, she changed the subject. "What happened to your wife?"

"Divorce. She couldn't deal with the PTSD."

As she ate more of her ice cream, Celeste tried to calculate how long he'd been out. If he retired from a civilian job, then he had to have been out of the military for several years. "How long have you been divorced?"

"Thirty years."

She whipped her head around. "*Thirty years?* And you've never remarried?" Then she realized how she must have sounded. "I'm sorry. I didn't... I just—"

"It's fine, Celeste. And, no, I never remarried."

She couldn't imagine how a man as nice and good-looking as

Thad hadn't found someone else in all those years. Were the women crazy or was there something wrong with him? She prided herself on being a good judge of character and what she had seen of Thad's let her know there had to be more to the story. She really wanted to ask, but didn't think it an appropriate thing since they had only met a few days ago.

Thad finished his dessert and shrugged. "I guess I never found the right one. But I'm still hopeful," he added, staring into her eyes.

Her pulse skipped. Celeste didn't know how to respond, so she said nothing and polished off the remainder of her ice cream cone. He stood, eased the napkin from her hand and walked the few steps over to a trashcan. For the first time, she noticed he had a slight limp. Had he been injured while serving or afterward? Again, she felt it too soon to ask something so personal.

He came back, extended his hand and helped her to her feet. "Is there anywhere else you'd like to go?"

"No, thank you." He tucked her hand into the crook of his arm and they headed back to where he'd parked the car. She and Thad spent the ride home conversing softly, interspersed with periods of comfortable silence.

Thad walked her to the door. "Celeste, I can't tell you how much I enjoyed your company today."

"I've enjoyed yours, as well."

"I'd really like to see you again soon."

"So would I. Would you like to come for dinner on Sunday, if you're not busy?" Celeste had no idea where that offer came from and couldn't tell who was more shocked, him or her.

He studied her a long moment, obviously sensing her hesitation. "Are you sure?"

"Positive." He intrigued her and she wanted to know more about him. "Is four a good time?"

"It's perfect. What would you like me to bring?"

"You don't have to bring anything."

"I was raised to never go to anyone's house empty-handed."

She laughed. "Same here. Maybe some wine then. I'm partial to something light and fruity, but get whatever you like."

Thad moved closer to her, leaving mere inches between them. "Something light and fruity it is."

She didn't have time to blink before his mouth came down on hers in a kiss that made her senses spin.

"I'll see you on Sunday."

Still reeling from the kiss, Celeste nodded and watched him stroll down the walk to his car. She closed the door and leaned against it, her heart racing. The man could kiss! She hadn't moved when her house phone rang. She had no doubts this time about who the caller would be.

"Hello, Deborah," she said when she answered. "Yes, we went to lunch and I just walked in the door."

Deborah giggled. "Well, don't leave me in suspense. How was it and are you two going to see each other again?"

She took the cordless into her bedroom, kicked off her shoes and reclined on the bed. "It was wonderful and so is Thad. And I invited him to dinner on Sunday."

Her sister paused. "You're going to cook dinner for him?"

"Yes. I don't even know where the offer came from. One minute we're talking about the good time we had and the next, I'm inviting him over for dinner. I don't have a clue what to cook." She hadn't prepared dinner for a man in years. It dawned on her that she had no idea what he liked or whether he had some kind of food allergy.

"Relax, sis. You're a fabulous cook, and I'm sure whatever you prepare will be fine."

"But what if he doesn't like it? Worse, what if I make something he can't eat. Maybe I should just call and cancel."

"Don't you dare cancel that dinner. Everything will turn out. Call Thad and ask if there's something he doesn't or can't eat. See, it's an easy solution."

"You're right. It's just that he makes me feel like...I don't know."

"He makes you remember that you're a living, breathing woman with very real needs. It's a good thing, Celeste. So, did he kiss you?"

"You are so nosy."

"Yep, I am. Now answer the question."

Her lips tingled in remembrance of the sweet kiss. "Yes."

"The sound of that yes tells me the man knows his way around a woman's mouth. And if he knows that, he—"

An image of his tongue snaking around the ice cream cone rose unbidden in her mind. "Okay, I'm ending this call."

Deborah chuckled. "Mmm hmm, you were thinking the same thing. Keep me posted and if you need me to help with dinner, let me know."

"I'll think about it."

"Seriously, sis, this is a good thing."

"I feel like I'm moving too fast."

"Says the woman who met, dated and married a man in less than a year. You, of all people, know that relationships don't have specific timetables. Just go with the flow."

Celeste sighed deeply. "I'll try." And pray she wasn't making a mistake.

Friday evening, Thad and Nolan stood in Brandon and Faith's kitchen cutting and seasoning the ribs and chicken that would be grilled for Saturday's baby shower. Brandon enlisted their help, as well as that of his mother and two sisters. The women focused on the decorations, while the men handled moving furniture and food preparations.

"I met someone this week."

Nolan paused in his task. "A woman?"

Thad nodded. "At the center on Tuesday. She'd come with her sister to one of the support groups." He shared the details of what transpired with Celeste, including the sparks of awareness he'd experienced. "It was the weirdest thing, and I kept telling myself I was too old for this sort of thing, but I know what I felt."

"Too old? If you're old, that makes me the same, and I can assure you Dee has no complaints." They laughed. "Hell, it's even better now in my opinion. You know, you haven't been serious about anyone since Annette."

He frowned at the mention of her name. He placed the seasoned chicken parts into the roasting pan. "I don't know why you're bringing her up." Thad had met Annette Cohen at a business conference a decade ago and they'd dated for six months before she decided she couldn't handle being with a man who wasn't "whole", as she'd termed it. He had gone out with a few other women who shared her sentiment, but Annette's words hurt because she had said just the opposite at the beginning of their relationship. He later found out that her circle of friends had convinced her that she would be better off dating a man without limitations. Because they worked in similar fields, Thad had seen her at a number of functions since then. The last time their paths crossed, Annette had hinted at a reconciliation, but Thad had no intention of starting up with her again. Men didn't want their hearts broken any more than women, and he was no exception.

"I'm just saying. Do you think this thing with Celeste will go anywhere?"

"It would be nice. I really like her. She's a widow."

"Does she know about—?"

"Not yet. She knows I served in the military, but that's all. We went to lunch today and she invited me over for dinner on Sunday. I plan to tell her then." If Celeste reacted the same as the others, at least he'd find out before investing his time and heart.

Nolan carried Ziploc bags filled with ribs to the refrigerator. "I really hope it works out. Speaking of women, how are you going to handle seeing Francis tomorrow."

"Same as always. I admit those old feelings crop up every now and again, but having my baby girl back has helped keep the anger at bay." When his ex-wife divorced him, she had taken their two-year old daughter with her. It had taken Thad twenty-eight years to be reunited with Faith. Francis had remarried and, as much as he wanted to resent the man who had raised his daughter, he couldn't. William Alexander had done a wonderful job raising Faith and she loved the man. Thad would never put Faith in the position of having to choose between them. He walked over and placed the covered pan on a shelf in the crowded refrigerator.

"You're a better man than me. I'd probably still be angry and bitter. But back to Celeste. When do you think we'll get to meet her?"

"You're dating someone, Unc?"

Thad and Nolan spun around at the sound of Brandon's voice and saw him leaning against the counter with a wide grin.

"Faith mentioned that you were talking on the phone to some woman and smiling about a date. By the conversation, I take it everything went well. So, I'll repeat Dad's question: when are we going to meet her?"

Thad eyed him. "Brandon, don't you have some furniture that needs to be moved outside?"

Brandon chuckled. "If you need some dating pointers, let me know." He gestured to his father. "Dad and Mom have been married too long, so he probably won't be much help."

"Contrary to your belief, I don't need any help. My dating game is just fine and has been since before you were born."

Nolan lifted a brow. "Boy, please. You act like we're near death. And as for whether I can't offer any help, ask your mother. I'm sure she'll tell you I'm more than able."

Brandon's face registered a mixture of shock and horror. He groaned. "Ugh, really, Dad? That's just too much information."

Thad and Nolan roared with laughter.

"What? You're the one talking about my skills. And how do you think you got here? Immaculate conception?"

He frowned as if he'd smelled something bad and held up his hands in mock surrender. "Just stop and forget I said anything. I'm out." Brandon pivoted on his heel and stalked out, muttering something about parents and being gross.

Still chuckling, Nolan said, "I bet he won't be offering any advice again."

"No, he won't. Like I said, I'm good on all fronts."

"Amen, my brother." They did a fist bump. "And I'll keep my schedule open for that double date."

"You do that." If things went the way he planned on Sunday, a double date would be just the beginning. He and Nolan seasoned another batch of meat and cleaned up the kitchen.

Faith came in as they finished. "Wow. You didn't have to clean up, but I really appreciate it." She kissed each of them on the cheek.

Thad noticed she had her purse. A quick glance at the oven clock showed the time to be almost ten. His brows knit together. "Are you going somewhere?"

"Yes, to the airport to pick up Mom and Dad."

"You're not going alone, are you?" Tomorrow would be soon enough to see his ex, but he'd push his feelings aside if Faith needed someone to go with her. He didn't want her out alone this late at night.

"No. Brandon is driving. Will you be here when we get back?"

"Probably not." He scanned the counters for anything they may have missed. "I have a few things to do tonight."

"Okay. Then I'll get my hug now." She embraced him and held on tight. "I can't tell you how happy I am that you're here."

She didn't have to. Thad knew exactly how she felt. "I'll be here a little early tomorrow, in case you need something."

"Thanks, Dad." She turned to her father-in-law and smiled. "Sorry, but Mama Dee said she wants to finish making the centerpieces and wrapping the silverware before leaving."

"Nolan shook his head. "Guess I'll make myself comfortable."

"I guess so," Faith said with a laugh. "See you later."

After she walked out, Nolan smiled. "Coward."

"What are you talking about?" Thad asked.

"You're just leaving because you don't want to have to deal with Francis tonight."

"No, I have to make a stop before the store closes." He'd invited her and William to the retirement party two years ago and they were cordial toward each other on the few occasions Thad had seen her, but he didn't actively seek out conversation. He'd see Francis tomorrow. Tonight, the last woman's voice he wanted to hear before going to bed was Celeste's.

CHAPTER 5

*S*aturday afternoon, Thad removed the last batch of chicken from the grill and carried it over to where DeAnna and Siobhan stood arranging food on a long table. He had no idea where they would put the large pan, but he handed it off and went to grab a beer. He passed Morgan and Kathi, Faith's best friend from Portland, coordinating a game that had to do with wrapping toilet paper around a person and shook his head. Before he made it to the cooler, he saw Brandon and Khalil standing off to the side.

"Brandon and Khalil, why aren't you two over there getting wrapped up like a mummy?" he asked teasingly.

Khalil snorted. "Please. There's no way I'm participating in that."

"Me, either," Brandon said. "First, they were crawling around blindfolded on a blanket with a bowl and spoon trying to scoop up cotton balls. Next, they're racing with an egg on a spoon, and now..." He gestured across the yard. "This. Nah, I'm good."

Khalil laughed. "True that, big brother. We're about to break out the dominoes, Unc. You want in?"

Thad grinned. "You'd better believe it. I'll be over in a minute."

"You going to get your crying towel?"

He leveled Brandon with a glare. "No, I'm going to get one for you. You didn't learn anything from last night about starting something you can't finish?"

Khalil doubled over in laughter and divided a glance between Thad and Brandon. "Last night? What happened last night?"

"Ask your brother." Thad chuckled at the look on Brandon's face. It was the same as the previous night. "Your dad and I had to remind him that we don't need any help when it comes to women."

"Wait. What?"

Thad winked and left them standing there, Brandon with a frown and Khalil with his mouth hanging open. He retrieved two beers and handed one to Nolan, then the two men joined the game of dominoes. Brandon and Khalil did lots of trash-talking, but Thad and Nolan ultimately came away as the winning team. Malcolm, Omar and Siobhan's husband, Justin, declined a seat at the table, leaving the two older men with bragging rights until the next time.

"The only reason we aren't playing is because it's time to eat," Malcolm said.

Nolan smiled knowingly and pushed back from the table. "Whatever you say, son."

Still laughing, they filed over and filled their plates with the many offerings. Thad sat at a table with Faith, Brandon, Kathi, Nolan, Dee, Francis and William. He'd been to nearly every Gray family function for almost forty years and, for the first time felt the pang of singleness. Immediately, his thoughts went to Celeste. He had no doubt she would fit in well. He realized he might be getting ahead of himself and refocused on the conversation flowing around the table. At the end of the meal, he went to dispose of his plate.

"Thad, can I talk to you for a few minutes?"

He shifted to face Francis and studied the nervous expression she wore. "Is everything okay? You're not sick, are you?" Faith would be devastated if something happened to her mother.

"No, no, it's nothing like that."

Thad hesitated briefly, then gestured her toward the patio door. "We can talk inside." Once they entered the family room, she sat on the sofa and he took the opposite chair. She didn't say anything for several seconds and averted her gaze. "What's on your mind, Francis?"

Finally, Francis glanced his way. "I owe you an apology, more than an apology, really."

He went still.

"I am *so* sorry for everything I put you through, Thad. You didn't deserve it and I know I'll never be able to make up for what I've done."

Thad always wondered whether she would ever apologize and had considered all the things he'd say. All the ways he'd unleash his anger on her. Now that the time was here, the bitter words would not come. His mouth settled in a grim line. "You're right, Francis, I didn't deserve it. And there's no way I can ever get back the twenty-eight years without my daughter."

"I know," she said on a broken sob. "I was wrong."

"Why did you do it?"

"I don't know what you mean."

He leaned forward and braced his forearms on his thighs. "Why did you wait until I left for my assignment, mail the divorce papers and take my baby girl away? Why didn't you tell me how you felt? We were together for almost five years and I thought we were best friends." They had met right after high school, dated and married within two years.

Francis swiped at the tears running down her cheeks. "I don't know. I was twenty-four years old and had no idea how to deal with what you were going through. The crying out at night and flailing around in the bed scared me and I didn't know what to do. The one time I asked you about it, you said you'd be fine."

Thad conceded her that point. Back then, he had been embarrassed by the nightmares and hadn't wanted to talk about them, fearing she would think him less of a man. "I should have told you about them."

Her soft gasp pierced the silence. "What are you saying?"

"That you weren't the only one who made mistakes. I could have dealt with the divorce, but not having Faith…" He closed his eyes to push down the rising emotions that always came with the memories. "Not having her nearly killed me."

"There's not a day that goes by that I don't regret what I've done, and I'll never be able to forgive myself for that. But I hope one day you can."

"I've already forgiven you. I had to for my sanity. The anger and bitterness almost ate me alive."

"Where do we go from here?" she asked, her voice barely audible.

"Forward. We can't go back." With that statement, the weight of his long-buried anger lifted.

"Mom? Dad?"

They both turned at the sound of Faith's voice.

Faith divided a wary glance between him and her mother. "What's going on?"

"Your mother and I were just talking, sweetheart. Everything is just fine."

"If everything is *fine*, why are you crying, Mom?"

Francis ran a hand over her forehead. "Faith, I just apologized to your father."

Her gazed softened. "I'm so glad you did." She stood between them and reached for both their hands. "So glad." Tears misted her eyes.

Thad was, too. "Did you need something?"

"Yes. We're getting ready to have cake and open presents."

He nodded. "We'll be right out."

"Okay." Faith kissed Thad and Francis on the cheek, then left.

He stood and extended his hand.

Francis hesitated a moment before placing her hand in his. She came to her feet and placed a hand against his cheek. "You're a good man, Thaddeus Whitcomb."

"Thank you." He started toward the door and she stopped.

"I need to freshen up a little first. I'll be there in a minute."

Thad watched her walk away and smiled, finally able to close the chapter on that part of his life. He'd told Francis they had to go forward and that's the direction in which he planned to proceed with Celeste. Something about Celeste drew him in ways he couldn't define. The only way to find out would be to continue exploring this thing pulling them together. He stepped back outside. Tomorrow's dinner couldn't come soon enough.

SUNDAY AFTERNOON, CELESTE HURRIED THROUGH THE HOUSE TO make sure everything looked the way she wanted. The beautiful roses Thad had given her had fully bloomed and she sat them in the center of the dining room table where she planned for them to eat. She'd taken out her good china and cloth napkins and set the table to her grandmother's exacting standards. She started to take a picture and send it to her, but that would open up a multitude of questions she didn't want to answer just yet.

Celeste went back to the kitchen to check the peach cobbler in the oven. Another ten minutes and it would be done. She'd texted him yesterday to ask about his food preferences, and he said he'd eat whatever she cooked. She decided on stuffed pork chops, sautéed spinach and some of the homemade dinner rolls her family always raved about. She had decided to go all out and homemade vanilla ice cream would accompany the cobbler. Celeste removed her apron and went to her bedroom to freshen up. As she applied lipstick, the doorbell rang. She peeked at her watch. Thad was fifteen minutes early. She did a quick spritz of her favorite perfume, smoothed down the peach-colored sleeveless dress and left to answer the door.

Her greeting died on her lips when she saw Thad. The man seemed to look better each time she saw him. Today, he wore a tailored gray suit that fit his six-foot frame to perfection. Realizing she'd been staring like a love-struck teen, she finally found her voice. "Hi. Come on in." She moved back for him to enter.

"Hello, beautiful." Thad handed her the wrapped single red rose and a small, thin package. "You look lovely."

He bent to kiss her cheek at the same time Celeste turned and their lips met. Thad took full advantage. Her heart skipped. At length, he lifted his head and smiled. It took a moment to clear her head from the sensual fog. "Um...thank you. And you didn't need to bring anything other than the wine."

"I brought that, too." Thad held up the gift bag." It's already chilled."

Celeste led him to the family room, pausing in the dining room to add the rose to the floral arrangement. "Please, have a seat." She gestured to the sofa.

"After you." He waited until she sat, then lowered himself next to her. "Whatever you're cooking smells good."

She smiled. "I hope it tastes the same."

"I have no doubts," Thad said, not taking his eyes off her.

Her heart rate kicked up again and she busied herself with opening the square gift to cover her reaction. She carefully tore away the paper and her smile widened. He had bought one of Brian Culbertson's CDs she didn't have. "Thank you, Thad." The temperature seemed to be rising by the minute and had nothing to do with the oven being on. Celeste jumped up. "Oh, I need to check on the dessert. I'll put this on when I come back." She held up the CD.

He smoothly rose to his feet and eased it out of her hand. "If you show me where your player is, I'll take care of it."

Celeste directed him to the BOSE system on the kitchen counter, removed the cobbler from the oven and placed it on a trivet. The music started and the sounds of piano floated across the space and she recognized the song, "Together Tonight."

"I love this song."

"It's one of my favorites, as well." Thad held out his arms. "Dance with me, Celeste."

The softly spoken request made her pulse skip. "Here? In the middle of the kitchen?" she asked with a nervous chuckle. She knew being in his arms for any length of time could be dangerous because it would remind her of how much she missed having a man hold her.

"Absolutely. We have everything we need—you, me, good music. It's perfect." He closed the distance between them and wrapped his arms around her. "Perfect," he repeated as he swayed slowly in time with the melody.

Celeste almost melted in a heap when he pulled her to his hard frame. Her arms raised up on their own volition and wound around his neck. In her three-inch heels, her head came just above his shoulder.

The man smelled so good, it took all she had not to bury her face in his neck. The light, crisp scent surrounded her like a warm summer day. Thad's voice broke into her thoughts.

"It's been a while since I've danced with a beautiful woman and I'm a little out of practice."

Celeste stared up at him. *Out of practice?* The sexy way his body moved against hers said he was anything but. "If you call this out of practice, I'd like to know what you're like when you're up to speed." She averted her gaze and closed her eyes. She hadn't meant to say those words out loud.

Thad chuckled and the deep sound enveloped her. "I plan for you to be right here when I do."

His hand made a slow path down her back, igniting a blaze as he went and Celeste sucked in a sharp breath.

He leaned back a fraction and looked into her eyes. "You know what that means, right?"

She was almost afraid to ask. "What?"

A wicked grin curved his lips. "We'll need to spend lots of time dancing to make sure I get fully up to speed. I don't want to miss a step with you." He resumed his close position and continued dancing.

Mercy! They finished the song without further conversation. When he released her, Celeste stood rooted to the spot for several seconds before turning to the stove. "Are you ready to eat?" Her hands shook as she went about removing pans from the oven's warmer drawer. She could feel the heat of Thad's gaze with every move. "I...I just need to put these on the serving plates, then we can eat."

"There's no need to do all that. I'll bring the plates from the table and we can serve ourselves in here." Thad quickly retrieved the plates and handed her one.

"You can go first."

He eyed her briefly and shook his head. "The lady always goes first, sweetheart."

The endearment, coupled with the low timbre of his voice had her emotions doing funny things. She placed portions of everything on her plate, took it to the dining room table and came back to get wine glasses. Thad followed with his plate and the bottle of chilled wine. She jumped slightly when his body brushed hers as he pulled out her chair. "Thanks."

Thad took his seat, reached for her hand and recited a short blessing. "Celeste, I really appreciate you taking time to cook such an amazing meal."

A playful grin tilted the corner of her mouth. "You might want to hold off on the praise until you taste the food."

"I'm not worried. I know it'll be as wonderful as the woman who prepared it."

Just like that, the heat skyrocketed. This man had a way of making her feel special, even though they had only known each other a short while. "I hope so." Belatedly, Celeste realized that Thad was sitting in the same chair Gary always used when they ate together. She had set the table by rote. For a brief second, feelings of betrayal surfaced, but she forced them down and reminded herself, once again, that the emotion had no place.

"Is everything okay?"

She glanced over and met Thad's concerned gaze. She patted his arm. "Everything is just fine." And it was. How could it not be, sharing a Sunday afternoon dinner with a gentleman? With him. Brian Culbertson continued to play while they ate and laughed. She found herself enjoying Thad's company more and more.

Thad leaned back in his chair and rubbed his stomach. "Celeste, you outdid yourself with this meal. And these rolls," he said as he popped the last bit into his mouth, "are to die for and almost melt in my mouth. What brand are they?"

She laughed softly. "Rolls a la Celeste."

His mouth fell open. "You made these from *scratch*?"

"But of course, darling," she drawled. She toasted him with her wine glass and took a sip.

He lifted her hand to his lips and placed a soft kiss on the back. "Smart, caring, beautiful and a fabulous cook. Celeste Williams, if you're not careful, I may never let you go." He picked up his wine and finished it.

Celeste almost fell out of her chair. She opened her mouth to say something and her doorbell rang. She frowned. "I wonder who that is. I'm not expecting anyone." She stood and Thad followed suit. "Excuse me for a moment, please."

He nodded and retook his seat.

As she walked to the front, it dawned on her that it might be her sister and vowed to wring Deborah's neck if she'd showed up to be nosy. Celeste sighed and opened the door. "Emery? What are you doing here?" She sighed again. She did not need this today.

CHAPTER 6

"*H*ey, Mom." Emery bent to kiss Celeste's cheek. "Did Aunt Deb buy a new car?"

Celeste angled her head. "No, why? And you didn't answer my question."

He gestured behind him. "I saw the black Buick in the driveway, and I wanted to see if you were okay." When she didn't move from the door, he asked, "So, are you going to let me in?"

"Now isn't a good time, but we can talk later. I have a dinner guest."

His eyebrows shot up, then he frowned. "You have a man in here?" Emery pushed past her and strode through the house with Celeste on his heels. "Who are you?" Emery asked Thad angrily.

"Emery!" Celeste snapped.

Thad came to his feet. "It's okay, Celeste." He extended his hand to Emery. "I'm Thad Whitcomb. It's nice to meet you."

Emery shook Thad's hand grudgingly. "Emery Williams."

If Thad was bothered by Emery's outburst, he didn't show it. In fact, he seemed amused. Celeste, on the other hand, wanted to smack her son.

"Your mother and I were just finishing dinner. You're welcome to join us."

"No, he isn't," Celeste countered, glaring at Emery. To Thad she said, "I'll be right back." She pointed toward the living room. Emery looked like he wanted to protest, but he must have recognized the warning in her eyes and thought better about it.

Emery faced Thad. "Will I be seeing you again?"

"Yes, and when we do, I hope we have a chance to talk."

"Oh, we'll definitely be talking." His jaw tight, Emery stalked out.

Celeste braced her hands on a chair and blew out a long breath. "I'm so sorry, Thad."

Thad brushed his lips across hers. "It's fine and I don't scare easily. Don't be too hard on him. It's not easy for a son to accept another man being with his mother, aside from his father. You two had a good marriage?"

"We did and I'll always treasure those memories. But he's gone now." She placed a hand against his dark cheek. "Thank you for understanding. You're the first man I've invited here."

"I'm honored and I'll do everything in my power to make sure you don't ever regret doing so." He smiled and gave her hand a reassuring squeeze.

Celeste returned his smile and left to deal with Emery. She found him pacing the living room floor. "Do not *ever* disrespect an adult in this house or anywhere again."

Emery stopped pacing. "But—"

She raised a hand to cut him off. "Do I make myself clear, Emery Jamal Williams?"

"Yes, ma'am," he mumbled.

"Good. Now, I'm going back to finish dinner with Thad. If you'd like to talk, you can come by tomorrow evening after you get off work. But you're going to have to check your attitude at the door." She placed her hands on her hips and waited.

"I'll be here."

She smiled and leaned up to kiss his cheek. "I love you."

"Love you, too, Mom."

"And stop pouting," she said with a chuckle. She hooked her arm in his and walked him to the door.

Emery stepped outside and turned back. "Do you like him?"

"So far," Celeste admitted. "We just recently met and it's too soon to tell the rest." Though parts of her had already conceded that she liked Thad *a lot*. "I'll talk to you tomorrow, honey. Drive carefully."

"I will." He hugged her.

She watched him lope down the walkway and laughed softly. His behavior reminded her of how he acted as a child whenever he couldn't get his way. She closed the door, exhaled and went back to the dining room. She stopped short upon seeing the cleared table. She found Thad stacking the dishes in the sink. "Thad, you didn't have to do that." Thad turned from the sink and gave her the knee-weakening smile that always did her in. The one that made her feel special, and the one that made her heart beat a little faster. "Just leave those plates right there and I'll take care of them later. I have dessert, if you're interested."

Thad's eyes lit with excitement and a hint of desire. "I'm more than interested, but I need some time to let all this good food digest." He pointed to the baking dish on the counter. "Is that a peach cobbler?"

"It is, indeed. I hope you like them. I probably should have asked first."

"It's my favorite, second only to a yellow cake with chocolate frosting."

Celeste burst out laughing. She didn't know what she had expected him to say—some fancier dessert or something—but not that simple cake.

"What?"

"That's such an ordinary dessert. I thought you'd name some lavish treat."

He grinned and shrugged. "I'm a pretty simple guy. I don't need anything complicated or extravagant to be happy."

Simple didn't come close to describing him, or his effect on her. "So, you're not a high-maintenance man, huh?" she asked teasingly.

"Nah. What about you?"

Celeste let out a snort. "Please. I don't have time to do all the things that come with being a high-maintenance woman."

He grasped her hand. "Then what do you say about two simple, easy-going people exploring whatever is happening between us?"

It took her a moment to reply. Just like the first time their hands touched, sparks shot up her arm. She needed to know why this man, and why now. "I'd like that."

Thad refilled their wine glasses, handed Celeste hers and lifted his. "To the beginning of something wonderful."

Celeste touched her glass to his and their gazes held as they sipped. "We can take these in the family room while we're waiting for our meal to settle." She led the way and sat on the sofa. Thad took a seat next to her and draped an arm across the back. He sat so close she could feel the heat of his body surrounding her. She couldn't help but wonder how this *exploration*, as Thad called it, would play out.

THAD WATCHED CELESTE SIP HER WINE. SHE LICKED HER LIPS AND arousal flared through his body. He took a hasty gulp of his own drink. "Is Emery going to be okay?"

Celeste waved him off. "He'll be fine. I told him to come by tomorrow and we'd talk." She placed her glass on the table and shifted to face him. "Today, instead of the twenty-nine-year-old he's supposed to be, he reminded me of how he was as a child. You mentioned having a daughter."

He smiled. "Yes, Faith is almost thirty-two."

"Then you know what I'm talking about."

His smile faded. "Actually, I don't. I didn't have Faith in my life until a couple of years ago."

Her eyes widened and a soft gasp escaped. "I'm so sorry. Why?" She shook her head. "If it's too personal, you don't have to answer," she added quickly.

"No, it's okay." Thad didn't speak for a few seconds as he pushed down the old pain that always surfaced with the memories. "My wife couldn't handle my episodes of PTSD, so after my leave ended, she mailed me divorce papers, packed up our two-year-old daughter and moved away. I sent letters for twenty-eight years, praying that my baby girl would answer." He recalled the devastation he'd felt every time one of them came back with "Return to Sender" written on the envelope.

Celeste covered his hand with hers. "How did you find her?"

"I had hired private investigators over the years to keep up with her mother's whereabouts. This last time, I had the man search for Faith. It took a little longer because my ex remarried and changed our daughter's last name." He told Celeste how he'd sent the box holding all of his correspondence, so Faith would know that he had never stopped looking for her. Then he shared the details of Faith's car accident when she had come to seek him out. "I didn't find out about it until she'd recovered."

"Is she okay?"

"Yes. And the young man who stopped to help her happened to be my best friend's son." Thad chuckled. "They're married now and due to make me a grandfather in a few weeks."

"That's wonderful. What about your ex-wife, do you still see her? I'd want to wring her neck every time I saw her if it was me," Celeste muttered.

"Back then, the thought did cross my mind. It's all water under the bridge now. It took some time, but I realized the hate and anger was killing me and I had to let go." Celeste stared at him in disbelief. "I had enough problems and couldn't afford to let the bitterness consume me. It took a long time, but I have my daughter." That Francis actually apologized still amazed him.

"I'm so glad she's back in your life."

"So am I. She's anxious to meet you."

"Is that right? I'll look forward to meeting her when the time comes. You said you had other problems. Are you talking about the PTSD?"

"That and the injury I sustained." Thad was hesitant to reveal the information because it always seemed to be the breaking point in his relationships.

Her brow lifted. "Something else?" She eyed him critically. "You don't look like...I mean." She cut herself off and a rush of color filled her face.

Thad placed his glass on the table next to hers and lifted his left pant leg. "I lost the lower part of my leg in Desert Storm." He waited tensely for her reaction.

"Oh, my word! You've sacrificed so much." Tears filled her eyes and she squeezed his hand.

He reached up and wiped the escaping tear from her cheek. "It's okay. But..." He paused.

"But what?"

"Some women don't feel they can handle being with a man like me."

Her face clouded with anger. "What does that have to do with anything?"

Thad didn't respond. For several years, his thoughts had mirrored those women—that he was half a man.

Another moment passed. Celeste angled her head. "Wait. Please don't tell me you think you're less of a man because of this."

"No, not anymore. But quite a few women do."

"That's a bunch of crap. Thad, just because you lost part of your leg doesn't change *who* you are. If anything, it tells me you are strong, brave and selfless. I can't begin to imagine what you went through and I pray you didn't have to do it alone."

He bowed his head briefly as emotions unlike anything he had ever experienced welled up with such force they stole his breath. Celeste was the first woman to tell him this. Words he'd expected long ago from the woman who had vowed to love him until death parted them. "So, it won't bother you?"

She rolled her eyes. "Were you not listening to anything I just said?"

He chuckled. "I heard every word, sweetheart." Thad stroked a finger down her cheek, then captured her mouth in a soft kiss. The mingled taste of wine and her unique sweetness filled him with pleasure. Shifting slightly, he drew her closer and deepened the kiss. She met him stroke for stroke, her tongue tangling and dancing with his. By the time they came up for air, several minutes had passed. He couldn't remember the last time he'd sat kissing a woman for any length of time. He glanced at her kiss-swollen lips and the rapidly beating pulse at the base of her throat, and had to look away.

"I think we should get that dessert now," Celeste said, her breathing still coming in short gasps.

Thad wanted to tell her she had already offered him the best dessert. Instead, he said, "You might be right." As much as he wanted to keep right on kissing her, he sensed something special growing and wanted to take his time and treat it as such.

CHAPTER 7

"I hope you're calling to tell me how fantastic dinner with Thad was last night," Deborah said when she answered the phone Monday evening.

"Goodness, sis. Where are your manners? No hello, Celeste, how are you doing? Just straight into my business."

She let out an impatient sigh. "Celeste, don't make me drive over to your house. You know I'll do it."

Celeste laughed. "Girl, you are too crazy. Yes, dinner was nice."

"That's all…just nice? I was waiting to hear about all the fireworks that were going on. He sure is moving slow."

"Oh, there were a few sparks, too." Every time Thad touched or kissed her ignited a blaze. The memories had kept her tossing and turning all night. "But I like that he's not pushing me toward the bedroom after two dates."

"He may not be pushing you, but your voice says you'd go if he asked. It gets all soft and dreamy," Deborah added with a giggle.

"Shut up." Celeste bit her lip to stifle her own laughter.

"You know I'm right. This reminds me of how you acted

when you thought you were in love with Michael Douglas in tenth grade—smiling all the time, looking all starry-eyed. You were totally smitten."

Celeste recalled her young crush and couldn't deny her sister's words. Michael had been the cutest boy in her class and they had dated for three months—an eternity at that time—before his family moved. She had been heartbroken. Though they tried to maintain the relationship, it faded shortly after. Thad made Celeste feel that same way. "I'll admit to being in love with Michael."

"And Thad?"

"It's weird, Deb. We've only known each other a week or two, but it seems like much longer. He's easy to talk to, makes me laugh, likes to dance for no reason, and—"

"Hold up. Dance? When did you guys go dancing? I thought he was only coming over for dinner."

"We didn't go dancing. I had mentioned during a conversation about music that I liked Brian Culbertson and he bought me a CD." A vision of the slow slide of his body against hers flashed in her mind. "He asked me to dance while we were in the kitchen."

Deborah squealed. "That is so romantic. The more you tell me about him, the more it sounds like Thad might be a keeper."

"Maybe. We like so many of the same things, and he's already asked me about going to a few summer concerts."

"Well, the calendar just turned to June and there are plenty to choose from."

"I'm looking forward to going." Celeste hesitated. "Deb, when he kisses me, it's like…I don't know."

"Ha, I do. It makes you want to get your freak on."

She could always count on her blunt sister to put it all out there.

"Don't get quiet on me. Go ahead and admit it, honey."

"Something like that," she finally murmured. "The only thing now is Emery dropped by and interrupted the dinner. He was not happy about seeing Thad."

Deborah snorted. "He'll just need to get over himself. I don't know why these kids think we're supposed to stop living when something happens. What did you tell him?"

"Nothing yet. He's coming by after work for us to talk."

"I hope you're not feeling guilty, Celeste."

"Emery looked so betrayed and the notion did pop up briefly, but I know there's no reason for it." And being with Thad made her forget all about the guilt.

"I'm really glad to hear you say that. Oh, before I forget, Trent said he'd go with me to the support group this week. We might even get TJ to go. Do you know if Thad will be there? If anyone can get TJ to open up, it might be him since he seems to know so much about the PTSD."

"I have no idea what his schedule is at the center, but I agree he may be able to help TJ since he's been through the same thing." Celeste stopped short of mentioning Thad's loss. "I have my biopsy tomorrow, so I won't be able to go with you, but I'm glad Trent will be there." Her mammogram had showed three calcium spots and, although the radiologist said it could be nothing, he wanted to make sure of it, instead of waiting to see for another year. The stereotactic biopsy would be done with just a local anesthetic and they would send the report to her primary care physician for follow-up.

"Are you nervous?"

"A little."

"The radiologist didn't think it was cancer, so we're just going to pray that he's right."

Celeste was determined to hold on to that hope.

"That reminds me, I need to schedule my mammogram."

"Get it done, sis." They'd lost two aunts to breast cancer and their mother was a seven-year survivor. With that family history, both she and Deborah never missed an exam. The doorbell rang. "Deb, Emery's here. I'll call you tomorrow to see how the session went."

"Okay. Night."

"Good night." Celeste disconnected and went to open the door. Though her son had a key, he knew not to use it unless he had permission or in case of an emergency. She chuckled inwardly. Emery wore the same expression he had yesterday. "Hey, son."

"Hi, Mom." Emery bent to kiss her cheek and entered.

"I'm having a grilled chicken salad and you're welcome to have some, if you like." She headed toward the kitchen.

"No. Thanks." He opened the refrigerator, took out the pitcher of iced tea and poured himself a glass. After returning the container, he slid into one of the chairs at the kitchen table.

Celeste sat next to him. "You wanted to talk?"

For a moment, he sipped his tea and said nothing. "I don't like the fact that another man was in Dad's house."

"*My* house," she corrected. "Your father has been gone for four years."

Emery placed the glass on the table with a thud. "But you're bringing all these strange men in the house now."

She shook her head and sighed. "How many men have you seen here? None. Because there haven't been any. Thad is the first man I've invited to dinner, and whomever I ask is my business. In case you don't remember, I'm your mother and a grown woman. I don't need your permission."

He released a deep sigh. "It's like you've forgotten all about Dad. I mean, look at you. You cut your hair and you've been traveling everywhere. You're changing, Mom."

Celeste stared at him incredulously. "Changing? This isn't the first time I've cut my hair, but now you have a problem with it? Let me ask you something, Emery. Do you ever go to the grocery store and pick up a quart of double fudge brownie ice cream because you know it's his favorite, then get all the way to the checkout before you remember he's not here to eat it? Have you ever woken up on a Sunday morning, gone into the kitchen thinking you'd surprise him with a special breakfast, only to realize your footsteps are the only ones in the house?" Her voice rose with each question.

"Mom—" Emery stood.

"No! *Sit* down and listen. I have not forgotten your father. I remember him more often than you'll ever know, and those are the times that are hardest." She took a deep breath. "Emery, I loved your father more than life, but he is gone. Am I supposed to lock myself in this house and wither away until it's my time to die? Is that what you're doing…sitting in your condo night after night waiting for your time to come?"

His jaw tightened but he remained silent.

"The night before your father died, he me made promise to keep living. I didn't think I would ever be able to, and for a long time, I didn't want to." Celeste had lain in bed night after night, sobs racking her body, wondering if the pain would ever subside enough for her to make it through one more day. At one point it had become so unbearable that she had wanted to die, too.

Emery lowered his head. "I never knew that. Why didn't you tell me, Mom?" he asked quietly.

"You never asked how I felt. You were wrapped up in your own grief and I did what women and mothers always do— buried my own pain to stay strong for you." She could see his pain and ran a loving hand over his head. "I'm finally able to live again and I have to keep doing it."

Emery buried his head in his hands. "I'm sorry. And you're right." He leaned back in the chair. "I guess I was just shocked to see another man sitting where Dad always sat." He dragged a hand down his face. "Where did you meet him?"

"At a mental health center for veterans. I went with your aunt."

"Did TJ go?"

"No. She's hoping he will soon."

He nodded. "I should call him and see if he wants to hang out. I tried when he first came home, but he sort of blew me off."

Celeste stood and went to assemble her salad. "He's having a hard time." The two cousins, though five years apart, grew up as close as brothers.

"I'll try again. Do you like him?"

It took Celeste a second to realize he'd meant Thad. "Yes. He's very nice."

"Well, if he hurts you, he'll have to answer to me."

She glanced over her shoulder and laughed. "It may not come to anything, so hold off." She added salad dressing and came back to the table. "And you weren't very respectful yesterday."

Emery groaned. "I know. I'm sorry for that, too. I should probably apologize the next time I see him."

"Yes, you probably should."

He shook his head and smiled. "How is it that you always get me to do something and make it seem like it was my idea?"

She patted his hand and winked. "Because I'm the mama."

"Yeah, yeah, okay." He picked up his glass and finished the tea. "I need to go home and get some work done. We're developing some new software and there are a couple of things I'd like to add tonight." He worked as a software developer.

"Okay. Don't stay up too late. You tend to lose track of time when you're on that computer."

He grinned and stood. "I have to be at work at seven tomorrow and you know my brain doesn't function well without sleep." Growing up, if Emery didn't get at least seven hours of sleep each night, he was grouchy and irritable for the entire day.

"I'm just glad I don't have to deal with your moods anymore."

"That's cold, Mom."

Celeste smiled. "Maybe so, but it's the truth."

"Don't get up," Emery said when she made a move to stand.

"I'll lock the door. Please pass along my apologies to Mr. Whitcomb and let him know I'll be doing it in person the next time we meet." He bent and placed a kiss on her temple.

"I will."

"Love you."

"Love you, too. Be safe."

"Always."

She watched him walk out of the kitchen, her smile still in place. She was glad they'd been able to clear the air because she didn't plan to stop dating Thad. As soon as she finished eating, her phone rang. Seeing Thad's name on the display had her heart beating a little faster.

"Hi, Thad."

"Hey, Celeste. I'm calling to see how things went with Emery."

"They went fine. He asked me to pass on his apology and said he'd do it in person next time."

"I'll look forward to it. I didn't catch you at a bad time, did I?"

"Not at all."

"Good. I was hoping we could talk for a while."

"Is there something specific you'd like to talk about?"

"Everything and nothing. I do want to ask if you'd like to go see Damien Escobar this Thursday evening."

"The violinist? He is such a talented young man. I'd love to go."

"Would you be okay with Nolan and DeAnna joining us? They're anxious to meet you."

While they ate the peach cobbler and ice cream last night, she remembered him mentioning them as the friends that had been there for him during his dark days. What had he told them about her? "I don't mind. I haven't double-dated in ages."

"That makes two of us. The concert is in San Diego, so we're hoping to leave midday to avoid some traffic and be able to have dinner beforehand."

The concert would most likely end late and she speculated on what plans he had made. "Are we spending the night?"

"No. We'll drive back afterward. But I would like to take you back for the San Diego Jazz Festival at the end of the month, the last weekend in June to be exact. For that one, it'll be just you and me, and I'd like to stay for all three days."

Celeste didn't know what to say. The parts of her that enjoyed concerts were ready to throw caution to the wind and say, "Let's do it." The smaller parts that hadn't spent more than a few hours with a man over the past few years were decidedly anxious. A weekend meant more than a passing fling. She couldn't imagine a man spending that kind of money on someone they only planned to date a few times. Would he book separate rooms, or did he expect them to share a room? And would she say no to staying in the same room?

"Celeste?"

Thad's voice brought her back to the conversation. "I'm here." She decided to take a page out of Deborah's book and go for it. "I'd love to go." She thought back on her sister's response when Celeste told her how Thad's kisses affected her. *It makes you want to get your freak on.* Something told Celeste, no matter the sleeping arrangements, they would end up exactly as Deb said.

TUESDAY, THAD HID HIS DISAPPOINTMENT WHEN CELESTE DIDN'T show up for the support group meeting. However, he was glad to see her sister enter with two men who he assumed to be her husband and son. He studied the younger man's slouched posture and tight features. Thad knew the look well. As Deborah took her seat, she smiled Thad's way. He nodded in acknowledgement. He checked his watch, then stood in the front of the room. "If you all would take your seats, we can get started." He waited until everyone had settled down and quieted before speaking. "You're all here because you or someone you love is suffering from PTSD. It can be overwhelming and the changes, frightening. We want you to know that you aren't helpless and you aren't alone. With assistance, you and your loved ones can work toward a more productive life." Thad shared the various programs and groups the center offered and stepped aside for Phillip to discuss how treatment options could minimize problems in relationships, careers and in school. Afterwards, he invited those in attendance to share what they hoped to learn.

Thad waited to see if someone from Deborah's family would say something, but they didn't. When the session ended, he spent a few minutes congratulating a young woman who had been attending the center for four months after her discharge from the Army. She had learned to manage her triggers and had recently opened up to her fiancé about them. Once she left, Thad made his way over to where Deborah and her family stood waiting.

Deborah greeted Thad with a smile. "Hi, Thad. I was hoping you'd be here today."

"I'm glad you came back."

"This is my husband, Trent, and our son, TJ," she said, gesturing to each man.

Thad extended his hand. "It's good to meet you, Trent."

"Same here. It seems like you all are doing good work here. I like what I heard so far."

"If you have any questions, be sure to let me know." He focused on the younger man. "It's good to meet you, too, TJ. I hope you'll consider joining one of the other groups."

TJ snorted. "For what? This isn't going to be any different than those other places. They start off all nice and the next thing you know, the only thing they're doing is handing you a prescription." He looked Thad up and down with disdain. "And why do you care? You don't know anything about what I'm going through."

"Son, watch your mouth," Trent warned.

Thad smiled inwardly. TJ reminded him so much of himself right after his discharge. "TJ, I know more about it than I ever wanted. How about you and I go talk while your parents finish up here, and I'll share with you what I know?"

TJ studied Thad for a long moment, a mixture of defiance and curiosity in his expression. Finally, he nodded.

"TJ and I will be in the dining hall right down the way," Thad said to Trent and Deborah. Seeing their concern, he added, "We'll be fine." He waited until they joined the group of parents heading over to the refreshment table and then led the young man out. Once in the dining room, he pointed out the variety of available snacks and drinks. "Would you like anything?"

"No, thanks." TJ dropped down into a chair at the nearest table.

He pulled out the chair opposite him, sat and waited.

"You said you know what I'm going through. Are you some shrink they hired to get me to talk about my feelings?" That last word held a note of sarcasm.

"I'm not a psychologist. My degree is actually in business. I know what you're going through because I've been where you are and worse." He shifted in his seat and slid up his pant leg. "Desert Storm."

TJ straightened in his seat.

"I was one of the lucky ones that day."

"You do know." He paused. "Do they ever go away?"

"You mean the nightmares?"

He nodded.

"With time. The memories will stay with you and you learn to manage them, but you can't do it alone. Believe me, I tried."

"I get so frustrated sometimes because the least little thing sets me off and I can't explain why," he said emotionally. "I see the looks in my parent's eyes and feel like I'm a disappointment to them."

"TJ, your parents love you and just from talking with your mother, I know that's not how she sees you. I'd venture to say the same about your father. More than anything, they're probably feeling helpless because they don't know how to make it better." Thad listened to TJ pour out his heart. He didn't talk, just sat and listened. The emotional battle he'd been dealing with sounded so familiar, Thad couldn't help but be moved. He rose to grab a box of tissues and placed them on the table.

TJ snatched a few out and hastily wiped his face. "Do you think I could call you sometime…you know, just to talk?"

Before he could finish his sentence, Thad removed a card from his wallet and slid it across the table. "Anytime, son. I want to encourage you to talk to your parents, too. Let them know the things that set you off—sounds, smells, anything. They want to be there for you, so let them."

He nodded. "Thanks."

"I'm going to find your parents. You can join us when you're ready."

"Okay."

Thad wound his way back to the classroom and spotted Trent and Deborah almost immediately. Deborah caught his gaze and rushed across the room.

"Is he okay? What happened?"

"He's fine." He waited for Trent to join them and told some of what he'd shared. "I encouraged him to talk to you about some of the things that trigger his flashbacks, and I think he will. He also asked if he could call me. I told him he could, but I want to clear it with you." Thad spoke directly to Trent. As a father, he could understand how the man might take offense to his son wanting to talk to someone other than him.

"Of course," Trent said. "We'll do anything to help him get through this. I really appreciate you taking time to talk to TJ."

"I gave my card to Deborah last week and I'm extending the same offer to you. If you have any questions, please give me a call."

Trent reached out to shake Thad's hand. "I just may do that. Thank you."

Deborah smiled. "I have a feeling we'll be seeing a lot of Thad, Trent. He and Celeste are dating."

Thad couldn't stop the smile spreading across his lips. Yes, that might be true for now, but he was beginning to want more than just dating.

CHAPTER 8

*C*eleste lay face down on the table in the imaging center with her left breast hanging through a hole as the doctor prepared her for the biopsy. She felt the sharp prick of the needle as he numbed the spot and tried to send her thoughts elsewhere. Every bad scenario played in her head. She couldn't have cancer. She couldn't go through that again. Fighting back tears, she pushed down the fear and willed her mind blank until the procedure was over. They had instructed her to wear a tight sports bra and she didn't know how the technician thought she could fit that ice pack inside, but Celeste made it work. "Now for the waiting game," she said under her breath as she drove home.

The doctor mentioned she might have some swelling and bruising and be sore for a day or two. However, other than a slight tenderness, she felt fine so far. Once she arrived home, Celeste ate a light lunch and sat out on her deck to read. Two pages in, her thoughts shifted to Deborah and whether she had been able to convince TJ to attend one of the support groups. Automatically, that made her think of Thad. They had laughed and talked on the phone for almost three hours last night. She leaned her head against the lounger and closed her eyes. Although she had been trying hard not to, she found herself comparing Thad to Gary. Where Gary had been more serious in nature, Thad had a great sense of humor. Gary had been gentle when it came to intimacy, but if Thad's kisses were any indication, she suspected he'd be much different. The thought both frightened and excited her. "You're getting way ahead of yourself, Celeste," she mumbled. She checked the time and figured Deborah should be home from the mental health center by now and picked up her phone to call.

"Hey, sis," Celeste said when Deborah picked up. "How did it go today?"

"Hey, Celeste. It went better than I ever expected. TJ actually went with us, and girl, Thad Whitcomb is a definite keeper. I don't know how he did it, but he got TJ to open up to him."

"That is fantastic news." She should have known that if anyone could get her nephew to talk, it would be Thad.

"What's even better is that TJ talked to us a little when we got home. He said he knows we want to help and asked us to be patient with him."

"Deb, you don't know how glad I am to hear this. Emery said he was going to call and see if they can hang out."

"That would be great. Just let him know not to take TJ to a crowded place or somewhere with unexpected loud noises. Those are things he confided that make him uneasy."

"I'll be sure to tell him."

"How did the procedure go?"

"Okay, I guess. I'm a little sore and I have to keep an ice pack on it for the next day or so. I just hope it's back to normal by Thursday. I'm going to San Diego with Thad and his friends to see Damien Escobar."

"Ooh, I love his music. He can play that violin. Are you spending the night?"

"No, but we'll be spending the weekend there when we go back for the jazz festival at the end of the month."

Deborah didn't say anything for several seconds. "Wow. I take back everything I said about him moving slowly. Now, *this* is what I'm talking about. We've got to go shopping for a few cute outfits to wear during the day *and* night. We also have to find some sexy lingerie to knock him off his feet."

"Who said he's going to see all that? He didn't say anything about sharing a room."

"Hmph. You're going to tell me that you can spend the entire weekend with that fine man and not want to get a little close up and personal?"

"Deborah!"

"Don't Deborah me, Celeste. There's no shame in admitting the man makes your blood boil. I'm not suggesting you sleep around with every man that comes along, but this thing with Thad is different. When I mentioned your name, his face lit up the same way Trent's does when I show up naked in the bedroom. So, if all it takes is hearing your name to get him going, imagine what would happen if he saw you in some sexy scrap of lingerie."

It didn't take much for her to imagine what would happen. She had sensed the deep passion in his kiss. "I can't with you, girl."

"But you can with Thad," Deborah said. "And you will. Mark my words. Sis, this guy is special and I have a feeling he's going to be around a long time."

Celeste let out a short bark of laughter. "How did you get all that from talking to the man for five minutes? And I've only known him for what...two weeks?"

"So. How long did you know Gary before you knew he was the one? Remember Mom and Dad met, dated and married within a month and they're still acting like newlyweds fifty-five years later."

Deb had a point. Celeste had known within weeks that she and Gary would be heading to the altar at some point. However, she had always believed things like that only happened once in a person's life. On the flip side, she could see herself and Thad in some kind of long-term relationship.

"No comeback?"

"No."

"I rest my case."

Celeste laughed and shook her head. "You are such a nut."

"Yeah, and you love me in all my craziness."

"I wouldn't have you any other way."

"Ditto, sis." They fell silent, both reflecting on their close bond. "Okay, enough of the mushy stuff. What do you know about Thad's friends?"

Still chuckling, she said, "Not much, aside from their first names—Nolan and DeAnna—and that they've been friends for almost forty years." Celeste had no idea of what Thad had told them about her. If they had been friends all those years, they most likely knew his ex-wife. Would they compare her to the woman? "I'm a little nervous about meeting them. Usually, you don't introduce a woman you've just met to good friends. That's something that happens a few months down the road. He also mentioned that his daughter is anxious to meet me."

"He has a daughter?"

"Yes. Her name is Faith and she's almost thirty-two. She due to deliver her first baby soon." Mentioning Faith brought back their conversation about his ex taking her away. Celeste got heated all over again, even though it had nothing to do with her.

"That's wonderful. How do you think she'll react to someone dating her father? She might see it as a competition or you taking her father away from her. Hopefully, she'll have more tact than Emery."

"I have no idea, and no one can be as bad as Emery. Thad said she wanted to meet me, so I'm going to take it as a good sign."

"Keep me posted."

"I don't have to because I know you'll be calling me Friday on your first break."

"Ha ha, what can I say? Gotta go start dinner."

"Alright. We'll talk sometime over the weekend." Celeste disconnected. She tried to read, but her thoughts kept straying to Thad and that upcoming weekend. Instead of worrying about it, she decided she'd go with the flow, wherever it led.

THAD'S CELL RANG AS HE TURNED INTO CELESTE'S DRIVEWAY Thursday. He engaged the car's Bluetooth system. "Hello."

"Thad, it's Dee."

"What's going on?"

"I know you had planned to drive today, but since you and Celeste are still in the getting-to-know-you stage, I figured Nolan can drive. That way, you can concentrate on your new lady, rather than the highway."

Leave it to Dee to still find a way to work on her match-making skills.

"I had nothing to do with this," Nolan chimed in.

"I didn't figure you did. This one time, though, I'm not going to argue with your wife. I'd take looking at Celeste all day over driving down a highway."

Dee squealed. "Ooh, I need to write this down. Thad, you've never agreed with me when it came to a woman. Hurry up and get here. I have *got* to meet Celeste. Bye."

The line went dead and Thad just shook his head. He loved Dee like a sister and didn't know what he'd do without her and Nolan's friendship. He got out and went to ring the doorbell. They had decided to dress business casual, but when Celeste opened the door wearing a pair of black slacks, black sleeveless tank with a sequined neckline and a sheer long-sleeved overblouse, it rendered him momentarily mute. Her soft laughter brought him around.

"Does that look mean you approve of my attire?" Celeste asked, doing a slow turn.

"I more than approve, and if we stand here one second longer, I'll show you just how much I like it." He leaned in and kissed her, trying to communicate exactly what he meant.

"I need to get my purse." However, she didn't move for a moment. Finally, she backed away and came back a second later and they were off.

Once they arrived at Nolan and Dee's house, the group piled into the Gray's Mercedes and headed out of town.

Dee turned in her seat. "I'm so happy to finally meet you, Celeste. We've been waiting a long time for Thad to find someone special and I hope we'll be seeing more of you. In fact, our family gets together about once a month on a Sunday for dinner and we'd love to have you. It's a big group and we always have a good time."

Celeste slanted Thad a quick glance. "That's very nice of you, DeAnna."

Thad leaned over and whispered. "I hope Dee hasn't scared you."

She held his gaze. "I don't scare easily."

Her statement brought back memories of when he'd told her the same thing. They shared a smile. Thad threaded their fingers together and made himself comfortable. The four laughed and conversed for the duration of the ride.

When they arrived at the restaurant for an early dinner, Celeste pulled Thad aside. "Nolan looks really familiar. I know I've seen him somewhere." She frowned as if trying to remember. "Maybe on TV or something."

"He did do a couple of commercials for the company, Gray Home Safety."

Her mouth fell open. "Wait, he's *that* Nolan Gray? And you worked—"

"As the executive vice president." Thad shared the details of how the company started in Nolan's garage after their discharge from the military due to the difficulties they had finding equipment and services for Thad. "He started designing them himself, I came on board after I was able and now it's grown."

"I'll say. It's one of the largest in-home safety companies in the country. You are full of surprises."

He smiled. A hostess came and led them to a table. Over dinner the conversation continued and Thad watched the interaction between Celeste and his friends. She seemed to like them as much as he knew Nolan and Dee liked her. If DeAnna didn't like someone, everyone around her knew it. The normally outgoing and friendly woman turned quiet and cordial.

"Thad mentioned you were retired, Celeste," DeAnna said as they ate.

"Yes. Six months ago and I am enjoying it."

"So am I. Before Nolan and Thad retired, they had to be dragged out of their offices."

Thad and Nolan stared at Dee and Nolan said, "That's not true."

Dee scooted her chair away from Nolan. "Let me move so I don't get struck by lightning from that lie."

Celeste burst out laughing. "So, you and Thad were members of Workaholics Anonymous, huh, Nolan?"

Nolan's brows shot up. "Oh, brother. Dee has found her partner in crime."

Dee pointed her fork in Nolan's direction. "Amen and hallelujah. Welcome to the club, Celeste."

"Glad to be a member, my sister."

Laughter broke out around the table and Thad thoroughly enjoyed himself. Afterwards, they drove over to where the concert would be held and found their seats. They were only ten rows from the stage in the center section. Damien Escobar hit the stage and put on a fabulous show.

Celeste leaned close to Thad's ear. "This puts a whole other spin on playing the violin."

"I'm glad you're enjoying the music." The young artist played pieces from several genres, including covers of Prince and Alicia Keys songs.

"Honey, I'm more than enjoying this." Damien started a slow ballad and Celeste reached for his hand.

Thad smiled at her, feeling a small tug on his heart. Their gazes held for a long moment, then she trained her eyes on the stage. He didn't let go of her hand for the rest of the show.

"He is so good!" Celeste said as they walked back to the car.

Dee nodded. "I know. I wish I could play an instrument."

"So do I. The only instrument I remember playing was that recorder in third grade."

Dee laughed. "Oh, my goodness. I forgot all about that. We had to learn how to play it, too, that and the autoharp."

Celeste chuckled. "Mmm hmm." Both women started humming "Jacob's Ladder" and pretending to strum the autoharp.

Thad and Nolan laughed.

Dee hooked her arm in Celeste's. "Honey, we have got to get together and have lunch soon. I haven't had this much fun in a long time."

"Yes, we will. I haven't either."

Celeste and Dee talked like old friends all the way to Nolan and Dee's house. After a round of hugs, goodbyes and a promise to do it again soon, Thad and Celeste departed. On the drive back, Celeste fell asleep. Thad stole glances at the woman who, in a short time, had him thinking about what he really wanted in his life. He couldn't complain because his was a good one. He'd been content with occasional dating, but as Celeste lay asleep against his shoulder, he could see them doing this for the rest of their lives. The thought shocked him for a moment, since they had only known each other a short while. However, life was not promised and he vowed to live each one of his days to the fullest. He now knew what he wanted and prayed it would work out as planned.

She woke up a few blocks from her home. "Mmm, I'm sorry for falling asleep. I guess I was more tired than I realized." Celeste stretched and shifted in her seat. "I had such a great time getting to know DeAnna and Nolan."

"They enjoyed you, too." Thad turned into her driveway, shut off the engine and got out. He helped her out and they walked hand-in-hand to her door.

"Would you like to come in?"

"Just for a minute." He followed her in, closed the door and gathered her in his embrace. "Thank you for making this such an enjoyable evening."

Celeste wrapped her arms around his neck. "Thanks for the invite. I can't wait to do it again."

He lowered his head and trailed kisses from her temple to her jaw. "Neither can I." He covered her mouth in a gentle kiss, infused with all the passion that had been steadily rising from the moment they'd met. His hands roamed down her back and over her hips, and he pulled her soft curves closer to the fit of his body. She moaned and the soft sound spiked his arousal. Thad wanted nothing more than to make love to her, but they were still getting to know each other and he didn't want her to assume this was nothing more than a physical thing. He knew where he wanted the relationship to go. He could wait.

CHAPTER 9

*C*eleste sat in her primary care doctor's office waiting for the woman to come in with the results of her biopsy. She had awakened that morning with memories of her wonderful night, and then the phone rang and erased her good mood. The fact that she hadn't been given the information over the phone worried Celeste. If everything had come out clear, she wouldn't have been given a same day appointment. The door opened and she jumped slightly.

The doctor entered with a smile. "Good afternoon, Celeste."

"Good afternoon, Dr. Banos."

She nervously bounced her leg while the doctor logged onto the computer. As the seconds ticked off, Celeste did all she could not to ask the woman to hurry up.

Dr. Banos perched on the stool. "The result of your biopsy shows atypical ductal hyperplasia. That's not a form of breast cancer, but it's a marker for an increased chance of developing it in the future." She provided a detailed explanation.

Celeste's heart pounded in her chest. "What happens now?"

"The recommendation is for you to have a surgical biopsy to

remove the cells, however, I want to refer you to an oncologist, as well."

"I thought you said it wasn't cancer."

"It doesn't show that it is, but we won't know for sure until after the test. I'd rather have all the pieces in place beforehand. Just in case."

She sat stunned for a moment. A sharp sense of déjà vu rose inside her and she fought to push it back down.

The doctor clicked a few keys. "I'll be right back." She left, came back and handed Celeste two sheets of paper. "These are the referrals for the biopsy and the oncologist. Come on out to the front and I'm going to have Greta call right now to get you on the schedule."

Celeste slowly stood and followed her out. Fifteen minutes later, she drove home, numb. Everything had been going so well, and now this. She knew Deborah would be waiting for an update and checked the time. Seeing that it was past the time when her sister got off work, she dropped down on the bed and pushed the button on her cell.

"Hey, sis," Deborah said when she answered.

"Hey. I got the results back from the biopsy and they found some pre-cancer cells. The doctor already scheduled me to meet with the breast surgeon and oncologist."

"I'm so sorry, Celeste. I know that wasn't the news you were hoping for, but I'm glad it isn't cancer."

"But some of those cells could be hiding." She blew out a long breath. "I have to tell Emery and I know he's going to worry."

"I can see that because of what happened with his dad. I know our family history doesn't make this easy, but I truly believe they aren't going to find anything."

"Our history is what has me worried."

"I hear you. Have you told Thad?"

"No. I don't want to worry him."

"Girl, you need to tell him. He'll probably want to be there."

"I can't put him through that." She remembered how it was with Gary—all the treatments, the pain, the bleak look in his eyes—and she couldn't subject Thad to the same thing.

"I still think you need to tell Thad."

"I'll think about it. I need to get off and call Emery."

"Okay, keep me posted. Hang in there, honey. It'll all turn out alright."

"I will and I hope so." They spoke a minute longer, then said goodbye. Celeste called Emery and asked him to stop by tomorrow.

She spent a restless night visualizing every possible situation, none of them positive, and by morning, her stomach was tied in knots. Her mother had gone through a similar situation and there had been a few malignant cells. Yes, her mother had come through fine, but Celeste would just rather skip the whole ordeal. Her thoughts shifted to Thad. Though she told Deborah she would think about telling him, Celeste had all but decided not to share the information with him. She laid in bed a while longer, then got up to start her day. Emery would be over around four and that gave her plenty of time to do her grocery shopping and cleaning.

As she went about her tasks, she couldn't stop her mind from racing. Celeste finished folding and putting away her clothes, then decided to call her mother.

"Hey, Celeste," her mother said.

Celeste smiled. Her seventy-two-year-old mother had gotten a smartphone and loved being able to see the caller's name on the display. "Hi, Mom. You have a minute?"

"Of course, baby. Is something bothering you? You never ask me if I have time unless that's the case."

"I had a mammogram and a biopsy and they found some pre-cancer cells. Now the doctor wants me to have a surgical biopsy."

"Oh, honey. I know you're thinking it's going to turn out like mine, but that may not be the case. Don't go borrowing any trouble from tomorrow. Today has enough of its own."

She sighed. "I know. I'm trying, but it's hard not to think about all the bad scenarios."

"What's your doctor saying?"

"She doesn't think they're cancerous as far as she can tell."

"Then we'll go with that. You're going to be just fine, Celeste. I can feel it."

Celeste laughed. Talking to her mother always lifted her spirits. "Thanks, Mom."

"Hey, that's what we mothers do. What else is going on?"

"Well, I met a man."

Her mother fell silent for a moment. "Really?"

"Yes. His name is Thad Whitcomb and he's pretty nice."

"Handsome?"

"Yes, he is." She told her mother how they met and about their subsequent dates. "Emery showed up when Thad was here for dinner and he wasn't too happy."

"He'll be alright. It's time for him to learn that life goes on. Send me a picture of Thad."

"Mom, I don't have any."

"Why not? Isn't that what all these fancy phones are for? I need to check him out and see if he's as handsome as you say."

Celeste burst out laughing. "I think it's time for us to end this call."

"Okay. Your dad and I are going to take a walk before it gets too late. Keep me posted on both things."

"I will. Love you, Mom."

"Love you too, baby."

She hung up and shook her head. Her mother could be outrageous and Deborah had inherited that same sassiness. She stood, grabbed her list and headed to the grocery store.

Emery arrived at exactly four and Celeste couldn't resist

teasing him. "I can't believe you're here. You've never been on time for anything, except work."

Chuckling, he bent to kiss her cheek. "Yeah, well, this sounded pretty important. Believe me, I thought about showing up two hours ago."

"Come on in and let's talk about it. You want me to fix you something to eat?" she asked as they walked through the dining room and kitchen to the family room.

"No, thanks. I met a friend for lunch."

"That friend wouldn't by chance happen to be a woman, would it?"

Emery groaned. "Aw, Mom, don't start with the when-are-you-going-to-settle-down speech."

"I'm not. I was just asking. Why is it that you get to ask all about my business and expect answers, but I can't do the same?"

"I don't know what you mean."

She rolled her eyes. "Right. So grilling me about Thad isn't jumping into my business?"

A guilty expression crossed his face.

"Mmm hmm, that's what I thought. So?"

He dropped down on the sofa. "Yes, Mom, it was a woman. We met a couple of months ago at one of those business expos and decided to keep in touch. She was in town for her job, so we met for lunch."

Celeste sat next to him and tucked her feet beneath her. "Oh, she doesn't live here?"

"Nope. Philadelphia. She's cool and all, but I don't do long distance relationships. So, what's going on?"

"Well, I had a biopsy in my left breast and they found some abnormal cells. The doctor wants me to have a surgical biopsy to make sure—"

"Make sure it's not cancer," he finished grimly. He braced his elbows on his knees and cradled his head in his hands. "Do they think there's a chance it is?"

"They seem to think not, but we won't know for sure until they remove them." The tension rolled off him in waves and she knew what he was thinking.

Emery lifted his head. "Are you worried?"

She gave him a wry smile. "I'd be lying if I said I wasn't."

He nodded. "Me, too. All I can see is a repeat of what happened with Dad and I cannot go through that again. I'm going to trust that the doctor knows what she's talking about and that the cells are probably not malignant." He gave her a strong hug. "Don't worry. It's going to be okay, I can feel it. I love you, Mom."

"I love you, too, sweetheart." He always did his best to make her feel better. Even as a child, when she had a headache, he would come and massage her temples. She could barely feel the pressure of his small fingers, but, somehow, the pain would dissipate. "I made some chocolate chip cookies earlier," Celeste said, wanting to lighten the mood.

Emery's face lit with a wide grin. He jumped up and took off to the kitchen. He came back a minute later with five of the dozen she had made, one of them half eaten. "These are so good," he said around a mouthful.

"Five cookies, Emery?"

"What? They're good. I brought you one so you can't say I ate them all."

She snatched the cookie he held out and took a bite. "I didn't raise you to be this greedy."

"Maybe not, but you did raise me to enjoy good food, and yours is the best." He polished off the second cookie and winked.

Celeste shook her head. "I know you're trying to butter me up for something. Whatever it is, the answer is no."

Emery brought his hand to his chest in mock disbelief. "Mom, I would never do anything like that." He laughed so hard, he started coughing.

Smiling, she pointed a finger his way. "See, that's what happens when you don't tell the truth."

"I need something to drink," he croaked, and went back to the kitchen.

Still chuckling, Celeste reached over to answer her ringing phone. "Hello."

"Now that's the sound a man likes to hear when his woman answers the phone. How are you, baby?"

Her insides flipped every time Thad called her *baby*. "Hey, Thad. I'm good. What's up?"

"I just left from Brandon and Faith's and I wanted to know if it's okay to stop by."

"Sure."

"I should be there in about ten minutes."

"I'll be here." Celeste hung up.

"So that's what the goofy expression you used to tease me about whenever I liked a girl looks like," Emery said, reclaiming his seat and taking a sip of milk. "I take it that was Mr. Whitcomb."

"Yes, and I don't have any goofy look."

"Whatever you say."

"He's on his way over."

"I guess it'll be a good time for me to make that apology."

She smiled. "Yep."

"If I didn't know better, I would swear you set me up."

"Not this time. You heard the phone ring. He was visiting his daughter. She's expecting a baby."

"Does he have any other kids?"

"No, just the one."

Emery brought the glass to his lips. "So, you're going to be dating a grandpa?"

If he hadn't had that glass in his hand, she would have smacked him. "He'd be dating a grandma, if somebody would settle down."

He frowned. "I'm only twenty-nine."

"I was married and had a six-year-old by that age," she said sweetly.

"Ugh. I think I need another cookie."

Celeste watched as he unfolded his six-foot plus body from the sofa and disappeared around the corner. A few minutes later, Thad arrived. He greeted her with a kiss that weakened her knees.

"I've been waiting to do that since I left Thursday night. These sweet lips call to me." Thad brushed his thumb across her lips.

The contact seared her. "Um…hi. Emery's here."

"Good. Maybe we'll have a chance to talk."

Emery was standing in the family room when they entered. "Hi, Mr. Whitcomb. It's good to see you again."

"Same here."

"I owe you an apology for my behavior the last time and I hope we can start over."

Thad reached out to shake Emery's hand. "Apology accepted and we can absolutely start over. I planned to take your mother out to dinner this evening, if she's not busy. You're welcome to join us."

"I appreciate the invite, but I already have plans."

Celeste sent an approving smile to her son and a grateful one to Thad.

They hadn't been seated two minutes before Emery asked, "So what are your intentions toward my mother?"

She whipped her head around and skewered him with a look. She would have to remind him, yet again, that *she* was the parent and not the other way around.

Thad, on the other hand, didn't hesitate. He spoke to Emery, but his eyes never left Celeste's. "I like your mother a lot and I'm hoping we can build something long-lasting."

She took in his serious expression and her heart started racing.

"Didn't you just meet her a few weeks ago?" Emery asked. "No disrespect, but how do you know all that already?"

Thad laughed. "When you get to a certain point in your life, it doesn't take long to know what you want or *who* you want."

Mercy! Celeste needed a fan. The intensity in his gaze threatened to incinerate her. She knew she was falling for him, but this just tipped the scale further.

FAITH CALLED WHILE THAD AND CELESTE WERE AT THE restaurant and his first thought was the baby. "Is the baby okay?"

"Yes. I just wanted to let you know you left the books."

"I put them down to help Brandon move the table and walked off without them. Let me call you later. Celeste and I are out to dinner."

"Ooh, go Dad! Tell her I said hello. You should take her to the Santa Monica Pier afterward."

"You've got to go to the amusement park, too," Brandon said into the phone. "She'll fall right into your arms," he added with a laugh.

Thad chuckled. "Thanks for the advice."

Faith giggled. "Bye and have fun."

"Sorry," he said after hanging up. "Faith wanted to let me know I left something at their house earlier, and then she and Brandon decided I needed some dating pointers."

Celeste leaned forward and propped her chin in her hands. "So, what did they suggest?"

"They said we should go to Santa Monica Pier and the amusement park."

"I love the beach, so that's a great suggestion." She leaned back. "I can't remember the last time I went to the amusement park. I used to go all the time when I was a teen."

"Then how about we finish up and do that, too?"

"You're on."

They finished dinner and drove over to the pier. Celeste hooked her arm in his and they strolled along the path. The warm mid-June temperatures made it a perfect evening activity and the contentment Thad felt, immeasurable. As they neared the carousel, Thad slowed. "Would you like to ride?"

"Yes."

The smile she gave him made his heart flip. He paid the fare and they climbed on, opting to sit on one of the benches. Thad draped an arm around her shoulder and she leaned against him.

"This is wonderful. So many memories. Can we head over to the amusement park after this?"

"Of course. We can go anywhere you want." When the carousel came to a stop, he helped her down and they headed toward the park. Instead of purchasing the unlimited wristbands, they decided to pay for individual rides. "It's changed a lot since the last time I was here."

"It has. I think it's been close to twenty years since I've been here."

"It's been even longer than that for me. Where to first?"

"If you'd asked me that question when I was sixteen, we would already be in line for the roller coaster." Celeste shook her head. "These days, that Ferris Wheel over there is about my limit for height and speed."

Thad laughed. "Same here. My daredevil days are long gone."

"Amen. How about you and me doing one more daredevil stunt, grown folks style? That Ferris Wheel is calling my name." Celeste grabbed him by the hand and started in that direction, her laughter sounding like music to his ears.

From the top of the ride, they had a panoramic view of the coastline and because the sun had begun its descent, the multicolored solar powered lights made for a spectacular scene. It seemed as if everyone had the same idea of taking advantage of the great weekend weather. Afterwards, Thad and Celeste continued to stroll through the crowded park and shared a funnel cake.

Thad couldn't recall ever being turned on by a woman eating, but tonight watching Celeste lick the whipped cream had turned him on in ways he couldn't begin to describe. His body had reacted as if he were twenty years younger.

At the beach a while later, he stood behind her and wrapped his arms around her. She covered his hands with hers, and together, they watched the last few minutes of the sunset. He turned her to face him. "This summer is turning out to be one of the sweetest I've ever known. You take my breath away, Celeste." Thad captured her mouth in a gentle kiss, then took her hand and resumed their walk. Afterwards, he led her back to the car.

Celeste placed her hand against his cheek. "I enjoy being with you, Thad."

He kissed her palm. "And I enjoy you. Are you in a hurry to get home?" The dash clock read nine o'clock.

"Not at all. What did you have in mind?"

"It occurred to me that you've never seen my place, so I thought we'd go there, have some dessert and talk or watch a movie."

"Sounds good to me."

They spent the drive discussing their favorite movies. It occurred to Thad, that other than Annette, he had never brought a woman to his home. He opened the door and stepped back to let her enter first. He turned on a table lamp and led her through the living room and kitchen to the family room, stopping briefly to retrieve a container out of the refrigerator.

"You have a lovely home. How do you keep it so clean?"

"It's only me here, so it's easy." He gestured her to the sofa and sat beside her. He handed her the box. "I know how much you like strawberries."

Celeste opened it and a wide grin spread across her face. "I *love* chocolate-dipped strawberries." She slanted him a glance. "You didn't want any, did you?"

He laughed softly. "I had hoped to have at least one."

"Well," she said hesitantly, "you did buy them, so I guess you can have one. But this big one is all mine." She brought it to her mouth and bit into it. "Mmm."

She used her tongue to catch some of the juice in the corner of her mouth and desire hit him hard and fast. He sucked in a sharp breath. Thad endured the torture of watching her finish it. She picked up a second one and offered it to him. Instead of taking it, he held her hand steady and bit into it. Easing it from her grasp, he rubbed the berry across her lips and licked off the juice. They continued to feed each other with intermittent kisses until the box was empty. He set it aside and turned his attention to kissing and tasting her. He wanted to make love to her and sensed himself teetering on the edge of his control. "Sweetheart, we need to slow down, otherwise we're going to end up in my bed."

"I know," Celeste said, still kissing him.

"Are you sure? I can wait."

She placed her finger against his lips. "I'm sure. There's something I need to say first."

"What is it?"

"I don't want you to ever think you're a substitute for Gary. You're not. I enjoy being with you because of who *you* are. No one else."

Thad rested his forehead against hers. "I will admit the thought crossed my mind once or twice, but I didn't believe that was the case. Thank you for saying it." He stood, took her hand and led her down the hallway to his bedroom. Once there, he took his time exploring her body with his mouth and hands. He wanted their first coming together to be one neither of them would forget. He slowly undressed her, lowered her to the bed and kissed his way down, then up her body. Thad circled his tongue around her pebbled nipples and drew them into his mouth. Her sounds of pleasure sent his desire higher. He planted his mouth on hers in a hot, searing kiss. His tongue stroked hers while his hand found its way to the silken flesh between her thighs. Her hips rose and he slid one finger inside. He wanted her to be as ready for him as he was for her.

"Thad...*ohh.*" Celeste moaned and writhed on the bed. Her hands came up blindly to unbutton his shirt. She opened her eyes, then sat up and alternately licked and sucked her way across his chest.

Sharp jolts of electricity went straight to his groin. He rose from the bed to finish undressing and don a condom, then came back to her.

"I love the feel of your body against mine," she murmured.

"I love everything about yours." Thad positioned himself above her, parted her legs and eased himself inside inch by sensuous inch. He withdrew to the tip and thrust again. A tremor raced through him. Celeste arched her back and wrapped her legs around his back, meeting him stroke for stroke. He couldn't begin to describe the sensations she aroused in him. "Celeste, baby." Their passionate cries magnified in the room and he moved faster and faster. With every stroke, he felt a tug on his heart.

"*Thad!*" Her body trembled beneath his and she screamed out his name as she convulsed all around him.

Her tight walls clenched him and a rush of pleasure shot through his body. Thad's orgasm roared through him and he yelled her name. Any lingering concerns he had about being a substitute for her husband dissipated as she called his name over and over. He withdrew and rolled to his side, taking her with him.

"I think I'm satisfied," Celeste said with a tired chuckle.

He idly stroked her back. "But have you had enough?"

"For now."

"Mmm, I'll go with that." It took a while for their breathing to return to normal and Celeste drifted off with her head on his chest and her arm across his midsection. Thad glanced down at her and knew that regardless of the short time they had known each other, he wanted her to be a permanent part of his life.

CHAPTER 10

$\mathcal{T}$hursday afternoon, Thad finished his workout on the life cycle and saw Khalil coming toward him. "Hey, Khalil."

"Hey, Unc. How did the new pedal work out?"

"I like it. The slight curve really helps and I don't have to work so hard to keep the prosthesis in place."

"That's what I like to hear."

"How's Lexia?"

Khalil ran a hand over his head. "She's fine, but trying to get her to slow down is like asking her not to breathe. I just got her to agree not to go to the café two days ago." Lexia owned a café on the first floor of the building that housed Gray Home Safety.

Thad grinned. "Are you ready for fatherhood?"

"Yes and no. I'm excited about holding my son or daughter, but afraid I might do something wrong. I don't remember feeling like this with Siobhan and Morgan's babies."

"That's because you're only spending a small amount of time with them. When you leave, they don't go home with you. But you'll be fine."

"I know, but it would be nice if when they were born, there was an accompanying instruction manual."

He roared with laughter. "I'm sure you'll have plenty of help between Dee and Lexia's mother, as well as your sisters. There are enough women to give you more assistance than you'll ever need."

Khalil folded his arms. "Speaking of women, I heard you're dating someone."

"You heard right."

He smiled. "Oh, is she the one Brandon was supposed to be giving you pointers on?"

"Yep, as if I need his help."

"That's what I'm talking about." He and Thad did a fist bump. "When are we going to meet her?"

"Soon, hopefully."

"Now I know why you've been in here more often. Don't think I haven't seen you. Gotta up your workout regimen to keep it tight." Someone called out to Khalil and he threw up a wave. "There's my client." He clapped Thad on the shoulder. "Let me know if you need anything."

"See you later." Thad turned around and saw Nolan approaching.

"You didn't tell me you were coming in today," Nolan said when he reached Thad.

"I'll be gone for the weekend, so I had to get it in now."

Khalil passed them carrying an exercise band and medicine ball. "Hey, Dad. I guess I should put a sign out that says it's seniors day, huh?" he teased.

Nolan glared. "Don't you have some work to do?"

"Going," Khalil called over his shoulder. "Tell Mom hi."

Thad and Nolan shook their heads and chuckled. Thad asked, "Are you doing upper, lower or both today?"

"Both." They started with the lower body, taking turns on

each machine to complete three sets. "You know I really like Celeste and Dee has been talking about scheduling that lunch with her. Do you think it might lead to something serious?"

Thad moved off the leg press. "I hope so." He paused. "Is it crazy to fall for someone so soon? This didn't happen with Francis or Annette."

"There's a first time for everything," Nolan said with a grunt as he completed his set. "And remember I told you I knew DeAnna would be my wife before we were even introduced."

"I still crack up about that. You were full of yourself back then." He remembered it well. The two eighteen-year-olds had been on a two-week leave and saw DeAnna out with some of her friends. Thad couldn't believe it when Nolan walked right up to her, asked for her name and phone number, then spent the following week visiting her. After their leave was up, Nolan wrote to Dee every day and during their next leave, married her.

"But I got my woman. And I still have her."

"Well, I'm looking forward to the weekend and spending some uninterrupted time with Celeste."

"I know you'll do whatever it takes to show her you're serious."

"I absolutely will. I hope it all goes according to plan." Thad was falling for Celeste, and by the end of the weekend, he wanted her to have every reason to fall right with him.

CELESTE AND DEBORAH SEARCHED RACKS IN THE WHITE HOUSE Black Market shop the evening before Celeste's weekend trip with Thad. It turned out to be the only day they could coordinate their schedules.

Deborah pulled out her phone. "The weather in San Diego is supposed to get up to eighty with lows around seventy. That's perfect for an all day concert." She picked up a pair of denim shorts.

"I'm not wearing those."

"Why not? You have the right body and great legs, and they're in style."

She snatched the shorts and put them back on the table. "Yeah, for someone *twenty-three*, not fifty-three." Celeste found a pair of white crop pants with a matching camisole and sheer pullover top with three-quarter length sleeves. It would work for both day and night. She added two pairs of *decent* shorts and three casual tops, then went to the register to pay.

On the way out, Deborah said, "Now, let's go find the good stuff. Vickie's, here we come." They found the Victoria's Secret store and she immediately pointed to a mannequin wearing a barely-there bra and thong. "This right here would guarantee a good time."

"No."

She chuckled. "What about this? The front clasp will make it so much easier for Thad to reach the prize."

"Hmm" was all Celeste said. Thad hadn't seemed to have any problems releasing the back clasp on her bra. In fact, he had undressed her with an expertise of a man who did it for a living. She picked up a red plunge bra and matching bikini panties that had a keyhole opening in the back.

"Yep, he's going to love these." Deborah studied Celeste. "Are you ready for what may happen?"

More like what had already happened. She shrugged nonchalantly. "Sure."

"I have one piece of advice. Don't be afraid to tell Thad what you want. Chances are he's going to wait for you to say it."

"We'll see." Celeste was more than ready for a repeat of one of the most sensual nights she had ever experienced. Just the memory sent heat spiraling through her. She couldn't wait.

WHEN THEY ARRIVED AT THE SAN DIEGO HOTEL THE NEXT afternoon, Thad drove into the valet area and helped Celeste out. The bellhop rushed over to get their luggage. "I reserved a suite with two bedrooms, if that's okay. I didn't want you to be uncomfortable or assume anything."

Reason number fifty-seven why I like this man. "I think we're a bit past separate bedrooms after..." A rush of heat stung her face.

Thad grinned. "And I can't wait to do it again. This time will be even better."

Better? She had been blown away by their chemistry and couldn't imagine what would be better. "How so?"

"Because this time, I'll get to wake up with you in my arms," he whispered close to her ear.

Celeste went weak. He grasped her hand and led her into the hotel's opulent lobby. It didn't take long to get the key, and after entering the room, something inside her felt that this would be a turning point in their relationship. But, in the back of her mind, concerns over the outcome of her upcoming procedure lingered. Forcing the thoughts aside, she decided she would only focus on this weekend. She walked around the suite. He had gone all out with the accommodations—elegant, but modern furnishings in the living and bedrooms, and oversized tub and shower in the bathroom. "This is beautiful."

"I hoped you'd like it."

Celeste smiled at him. "Mission accomplished." Leaving the bathroom, she crossed the room to the sliding glass door leading to the balcony. "Wow. I love this view."

Thad slid his arms around her and pressed a kiss to her neck. "I know how much you like watching the water, so I wanted to make sure you had the best view possible. We're not far from the beach, so we'll spend time there, as well."

She had casually mentioned her love of the beach, but didn't realize he had been paying that much attention. "It's fabulous." She turned in his arms and kissed him. "Thank you for this."

"You're welcome. I want to do whatever makes you happy." He covered her mouth in an explosive kiss that stole her breath and stripped her sanity. When he deepened the kiss, it brought forth all the emotions she had tried to tell herself were too soon to feel. Everything he tried to communicate, she heard loud and clear, and she was helpless to resist. She didn't want to. Celeste gave in to the sensations coursing through her mind, body and soul. At length, he lifted his head.

"I know we haven't known each other very long, and it seems like it's all moving fast, but I love being with you, Celeste. I can see us this way for a long time."

What did that mean? As much as she wanted to know, part of her was afraid of the answer because it would require her to admit she had fallen for him completely.

A knock sounded, sparing her from responding, and Thad went to answer the door. The bellhop entered with their bags. Thad thanked and tipped the young man, then came back out to the balcony. "If you want to rest, feel free. Since we opted not to do the add-on concert tonight, I made reservations at Morton's for six-thirty."

"What time do you want to leave?"

"The restaurant is right down the street, so fifteen minutes before is fine. Is there something you want to do?"

A smile creased her face. "You mentioned the beach and I'd like to go for a little while."

He checked his watch. "It's almost three now, so if we got back around five, would that be enough time for you to prepare for dinner?"

"Plenty. I want to change really quick." Celeste had worn jeans, but the warmer temperatures warranted something lighter."

"I'm going to do the same. It's too hot for jeans."

"You read my mind." They shared a smile.

"Take the master bedroom and I'll use the other one," he said, carrying her bag into the room and placing it on the luggage rack.

She closed the door behind him and selected the white crop pants and top she had purchased the day before and matching sandals. When she came out five minutes later, she burst out laughing.

Thad turned from his spot on the balcony and smiled. "I see you got the memo."

"I guess so." He had on a pair of white linen pants and a white button-down short-sleeved shirt. They were still laughing about it when he parked in the lot at the beach. "This is such a beautiful day." The sun shone in a clear blue sky and a slight breeze blew.

"I agree." He brought her hand to his lips and placed a lingering kiss in the center of her palm. "But it's got nothing on you, baby." He entwined their fingers and gestured her forward.

Celeste's pulse skipped with the soft endearment. As they walked along the water's edge, she marveled at the contentment she felt with him. It seemed as if she'd known him all her life. She stopped to observe the waves for a while before resuming their leisurely pace.

"Penny for your thoughts."

"My thoughts are worth far more than a penny."

Thad laughed. "Okay, then. Ten dollars for your thoughts."

She held out her hand. "Pay up and I'll tell you everything you want to know."

He stopped. "Excuse me?"

"You said ten dollars for my thoughts." She shrugged. "I'm waiting on the money before I divulge my secrets." She cracked up at the stunned look on his face. Celeste gave him a winning smile and wiggled her fingers. It was her turn to be surprised when he pulled a twenty-dollar bill from his wallet and placed it in her hand.

"Double the money, double the thoughts."

Her mouth fell open.

"I'm waiting, Miss My-Thoughts-Are-Worth-More-Than-A-Penny." He folded his arms and lifted a brow. A smile tugged at the corners of his mouth.

She couldn't stop the laughter spilling from her lips. He joined her and the two of them stood on the beach doubled over. It had been a long time since Celeste experienced such freedom and peace. The man in front of her had a lot to do with it. She wiped tears of mirth from her eyes. "You are so good for me, Thaddeus Whitcomb."

A look of tenderness filled his face. "And meeting you, Celeste, has been the best thing to happen to me. Thank you for coming into my life."

"I wouldn't want to be anywhere else." The kiss that followed expressed every emotion she felt at that moment. His kisses had always been passionate, but she sensed something different this time. Something that let her know this was anything but casual. Desire raced through her and grabbed her with such force, her body trembled. She broke off the kiss and rested her head against his shoulder. Deborah's words came back to her. *Don't be afraid to tell Thad what you want. Chances are he's going to wait for you to say it.* Today, she would take a page out of her sister's book. "I'm ready to go back to the hotel."

Thad's brows knit in concern. "Are you okay?"

"I will be once we get to the room." Celeste saw the instant he understood. "We should probably push back those dinner reservations." They had been at the beach for less than an hour, but she didn't want one second of their time to be rushed.

He took out his phone at the same time he started walking.

By the time they reached the car, he'd accomplished the task. "I changed it to eight and that gives us an additional hour and a half."

"I'm certain that's enough time. For now."

"If it's not, there's always room service."

The heat in his eyes sent a sweet ache straight to her core. They couldn't get to the hotel fast enough. They barely made it in the room before his magical kisses began again. His tongue swept through her mouth, igniting a blaze that set her whole body on fire. She had no idea that he had unfastened her pants until she felt his hands on the bare skin of her hips and buttocks. He slowly caressed her spine, sides and breasts, lingering in some spots longer than others.

Thad trailed his tongue along the sensitive spot on her neck. "I can't get enough of kissing you, touching you."

"Then don't stop," Celeste said breathlessly.

"I don't plan to. Not until you tell me you've had enough... until you're completely satisfied."

Before she could draw her next breath, he picked her up, carried her into the bedroom and placed her in the center of the bed. She moaned as he kissed his way up her belly, pushing her top up as he went, and finally removing it. He undid the front clasp of her bra and cupped her breasts in his hands, kneading and massaging them. He took one pebbled nipple into his mouth, then the other, while his hand charted a path down her front to the softness between her thighs. Celeste's hips flew off the bed and she cried out from the exquisite pleasure.

"Raise up a little, sweetheart."

She lifted her hips and he pulled her pants and panties off. Lifting her legs onto his shoulders, Thad skated his tongue up her inner thighs then plunged into her wet heat. Each swipe against the sensitive flesh brought her closer and closer to the edge until an orgasm slammed into her. As she lay gasping for air, he left the bed briefly to undress. His lean, hard body belied his age. Her gaze traveled down his broad chest and flat belly to his full erection sheathed in a condom.

The mattress dipped as Thad slid in next to her. He lifted her to straddle him and lowered her onto his hard length. "We're going to take this nice and slow."

Celeste shuddered from his words and the feel of him entering her. The leisurely pace he set, along with his deep thrusts drew her further into his sensual web and she lost all sense of time and space. He slowed, then stilled. She whimpered.

Thad palmed her face and held her gaze. "This isn't sex, Celeste. This is a man making love to the woman who's captured his heart."

She gasped softly. She was still trying to process his statement when he began moving again. "Thad, I...ohh." Her words were forgotten as passion took over. No other man had touched her soul this way. Not even her late husband. Celeste leaned down and crushed her mouth to his. A low groan erupted from his throat and he quickened his movements. Abruptly, she broke off the kiss and yelled his name as her body splintered into a million pieces.

Without missing a beat, Thad switched their positions until she was flat on her back and thrust with long, languid strokes.

"Thad," she panted.

"What, baby? You want more?" He gripped her hips and increased the pace.

Her cries grew louder and her breathing came in short gasps. The pleasure started low in her belly and spread through her like a wildfire. Celeste came again, seized by sensations so strong she thought she might never be whole again.

Thad went rigid above her, then threw his head back and let out a guttural groan as he found his own release. "Celeste," he whispered, his body trembling against hers. He pulled out, collapsed on the bed next to her and held her in his arms.

Celeste's heart still raced. He said he wouldn't stop until she was satisfied, and her only thought: mission accomplished.

CHAPTER 11

$\mathcal{T}$ had glanced over at Celeste bobbing her head to the music Sunday morning and smiled. The past two days had been ones he never thought he would experience. He'd told her he loved her. Not in those exact words, but the sentiment was the same. He could see the same in her eyes whenever she looked at him, sensed it in every touch and kiss. However, she hadn't reciprocated. For the first time, he started to wonder if he had come on too strong. Thad hadn't meant to share what lay in his heart so soon, but the words refused to stay buried. He was long past the age of playing games—he never had played them—and he had one goal: make Celeste his…forever.

"I am loving this music." Celeste snapped her fingers and gyrated in her seat to the up-tempo piece being played by saxophonist Eric Darius.

Her movements brought to remembrance the way she had ridden him Friday afternoon. They never did make it out of the room for dinner. He wouldn't mind a repeat and his groin stirred in agreement. Though she seemed to be enjoying herself, something had changed between last night and this morning. Thad couldn't put his finger on just what it might be, but he'd seen the brief shadows crossing her face and sensed the tense-ness behind the smile. Did she have regrets? Was she feeling as though she had betrayed her late husband? He knew that some-times happened. Not wanting to speculate further or ruin what had been the best weekend he'd had in years, he stood and pulled Celeste out of her chair to dance along with the other people already on their feet. The smile she gave him went straight to his heart. Yes, he loved her, and he wasn't going to let her go. Not without a fight. They would work through whatever was bothering her.

During the next break, they made their way to the exit. He had already checked out of the hotel and the two of them agreed to leave for LA earlier to avoid some of the traffic. They rode the first several miles in companionable silence, the only sounds coming from the music flowing through the speakers. "Did you enjoy yourself?"

Celeste rolled her head in his direction. "I more than enjoyed myself. This was the best weekend I've had in a very long time."

"Same here. Is everything okay?" He glanced over at her briefly.

"Of course. Why?"

"I don't know. This morning you seemed a little down."

She waved him off. "Sad that the weekend is over, that's all."

She said the words, but they didn't sound convincing to his ears. Again, he wondered if him revealing his emotions had put her off. He opened his mouth to ask and his cell rang. Thad engaged the Bluetooth.

"Hey, Unc," Brandon said when Thad answered.

"Hey, Brandon. What's up?"

"Faith is in labor and we're on the way to the hospital."

"She isn't due for another two weeks."

"I guess your grandchild is a little anxious to get here," he said with a chuckle.

Thad's heart rate increased. He likely wouldn't get to LA for another couple of hours and he didn't know if he'd be able to handle not getting there in time. "We're on our way back from San Diego, so I can't be there right away."

"Don't worry, Dad. The baby and I will be here whenever you arrive," Faith said.

"How are you doing, baby girl?"

"Can't say the past two hours have been a picnic, but I'm okay. Just be careful driving back."

"I will. I love you, Faith."

"Love you, too." She groaned.

Brandon came back on the line. "I'll call you once we get checked in."

"Please do." Thad disconnected, his worry mounting.

Celeste placed a gentle hand on his shoulder. "Do you want me to drive? You look like a nervous wreck."

"No, I'm fine. Just praying that she and baby will be alright."

"I'm sure they will be. Two weeks isn't too early." She reached for his hand.

Thad held on to it for the rest of the nearly three-hour drive. "You don't mind going to the hospital, do you?"

"Not at all. I know you're anxious to be with your daughter. I'll be fine."

"Thank you." He parked in the lot and they hurried inside. Brandon had called thirty minutes ago to let him know that Faith still had a ways to go, but was hanging in there. He had also told Thad Nolan and DeAnna were in the hospital waiting room. Thad sent a quick text to Nolan.

A minute later, Nolan rounded the corner. The two men shared a rough hug. Nolan turned to Celeste and kissed her cheek. "It's good to see you again, Celeste."

"Good to see you, too. Congratulations."

"Thanks. This will be number four. Do you come from a big family?" he asked as he started walking.

"Not too big. I have one sister. Why?"

"I have to warn you. The Grays are big on family. I have five children and all are married. And they're all here."

Thad laughed and placed his arm around Celeste's shoulders. "They're a lively bunch and can be a tad bit overwhelming, but the love is genuine."

"Dee has already told everyone about you, so be prepared because they are all anxious to meet Uncle Thad's new lady," Nolan said with a wink.

Celeste's eyes widened and her steps slowed. "You didn't tell me I'd have to be interrogated, Thad."

He kissed her temple. "It'll be fine. I promise," he added at her skeptical look.

DeAnna rushed over to greet them as soon as they entered the waiting room. She hugged Celeste. "Hey, Celeste. How was the jazz festival?"

"It was fabulous." Celeste glanced around the room, then back at Thad.

Thad smiled. Every eye in the room had turned their way and all their expressions bore a look of curiosity as they called out affectionate greetings. He escorted Celeste over to where they sat. "This is Celeste Williams." He introduced her to everyone.

Siobhan, the oldest, rose from her seat and embraced Celeste. "We're so happy to meet you. Uncle Thad is special and I'm glad he's found you. We'll be having a family dinner at my parent's house two Sundays from now, so Uncle Thad will let you know the time and bring you."

"That's very nice of you to offer, but—" Celeste started.

"Oh, we're all family, so of course you have to come. If you need anything, just let Unc know. He has my number. You'll be there, right?"

"I—"

"Great." Siobhan gave her another quick hug and sat down.

Thad chuckled at the stunned look on Celeste's face. "Sorry, babe. Siobhan is the PR director for the company. She's very good at what she does." He gestured her to a seat.

"I'll say." Celeste sat. "This is a really big family," she whispered. "You're their uncle? I thought you said you and Nolan were friends."

"We are. I've been part of their lives from the time they were born, so they think of me as family." In a way, Thad was glad she had been able to meet all of them. If things worked out the way he planned, Celeste would become part of this family, as well.

She patted his hand. "From the way they all greeted you, I can tell they love you a lot."

He glanced around the room at the faces of the children he used to carry on his shoulders and his heart swelled. "I love them, too." However, nothing compared to the love he had for his daughter. As the minutes and hours passed, Thad found it hard to sit still. He had been out of the country when Faith was born, and the same helplessness he'd experienced then, seemed to magnify now. A touch on his hand drew him out of his thoughts.

"Babies tend to have their own timetables, and I'm sure Faith is doing just fine."

Thad kissed Celeste's hand. "I know. I just hate being out here and not knowing what's going on. Having you here with me means the world." Movement across the room caught his attention. Brandon stood in the doorway with a broad smile. Thad jumped up and rushed over, along with everyone else.

Brandon held up a hand to quiet all the questions being thrown his way. "We have a healthy baby girl. Mom and baby are doing fine." He shook his head, a look of amazement on his face.

"When can we see them?" DeAnna asked.

"Faith wants to see her dad first. Then we can do a couple at a time." Brandon clapped Thad on the shoulder. "Unc, she did good. Real good."

"Thank God," was all Thad could manage. He faced Celeste.

"Go be with your daughter. Congratulations, Grandpa."

Grandpa. The word filled him with pride. He nodded and followed Brandon down the hall.

Brandon stopped at a door and pushed it open. "Go on in. I'll wait out here."

Thad looked up at the young man who used to fit in his arms, but now eclipsed Thad's height by a good four inches. "I'm proud of you, Brandon, and even prouder to call you my son."

"The feeling is mutual, Unc." He embraced Thad, then gestured him inside.

Thad had no words for the intense emotions that gripped him the moment he saw Faith cradling his granddaughter in her arms. He crossed the room and bent to kiss Faith's forehead. "How's my favorite girl?" He sat on the chair that had been placed next to the bed.

Faith gave him a tired smile. "Exhausted." She glanced down at the tiny bundle and stroked a finger down the baby's cheek. "But she was worth every second of pain. Dad, meet your grand-daughter, Zola Sharee Gray." She carefully transferred the baby to Thad.

Tears of joy blurred his vision as he stared at the small face that reminded him so much of Faith. "Welcome to the world, Zola." He placed a gentle kiss on her smooth brown cheek. "She's absolutely beautiful and looks like you."

Faith chuckled. "Make sure you tell Brandon that. He swears she looks like him. She does have her daddy's eyes."

Zola studied Thad curiously, her light brown eyes an exact match to her father's. Thad couldn't stop staring at her. "Does your mom know she's here?"

"Yes. Brandon called her. They're going to fly down in a couple of weeks."

"I figured Francis would be on the first flight out."

She smiled. "She would've been if I hadn't asked her to wait. I told her I wanted Brandon and I to have some bonding time before she camped out at the house."

A pang of disappointment hit him at the thought of not being able to see Zola for the next two weeks.

"I also wanted you to have some extra bonding time before having to share her with everybody." Faith laid a hand on his arm. "I know it won't make up for everything you've missed, but Brandon and I agree that you can visit as often as you like during these two weeks. We're restricting the rest of the family," she added with a wry smile.

His daughter was going out of her way to make up for something she had no part in. Thad tried to speak around the lump in his throat, but could only nod. He held Zola a moment longer. "I guess I should let Nolan and Dee in before she has my head."

"You're right. My mother-in-law isn't the most patient person when it comes to things like this, but in a good way. I love you, Daddy."

Thad stilled. She had never called him Daddy before, just Dad. Hearing it made his heart swell. "And I love you, Faith. You are my heart." He stroked a tender hand over her forehead and placed a soft kiss there. "I'll see you later." He smiled as he left. His world couldn't be more perfect than if he had planned it himself.

Monday, Celeste sat across from Deborah at a café near Deborah's job.

"Well? Don't keep me in suspense. How was it?"

"Can't I even order first?"

"Multitask. We've been here several times and you almost always order the same tostada salad and iced tea, so out with it."

Celeste lowered the menu. "We had a great time and I had a chance to see many of my favorite music artists all in one place." The weekend in San Diego played over in her head, particularly some of the more intimate moments and the second visit to the beach Saturday evening. It was then that Thad had told her he loved her. He'd hinted at it during love-making the previous day, but hearing him say those three little words while standing on the beach under a star-studded clear sky had melted her heart.

"I know Thad enjoyed that sexy nightgown we picked out."

She pretended to study her menu. The short, revealing scrap of silk had never made it out of the suitcase. She glanced up to see Deborah staring at her with a knowing smile.

"The fact that you're silent tells me one of two things. One, you slept in separate beds—which I *highly* doubt—or two, Thad is the man and you didn't even think about that gown." When Celeste didn't say anything, Deborah laughed. "Just as I thought. Thad is the *man.*

Celeste took a hasty glimpse over her shoulder. "Can we not talk about this in public? Somebody might hear you."

She waved a hand. "Girl, it's only sex. People do it all the time, and now so do you."

Celeste frowned. "You make it sound like some one-night stand or casual hook-up, and that's not how it is." The words left her mouth before they registered in her brain. She didn't want her sister to know the depths of her emotions. Celeste hadn't made sense of them herself and, with her potential diagnosis hanging over her head, they wouldn't matter.

"You love him," Deborah said simply.

"What? I didn't say anything about love." The server came to take their order.

Deborah waited until the young man walked away. "You don't have to, sis. I can see it all over your face and hear it in your voice whenever you mention his name. I am so happy for you."

Celeste's cell rang and interrupted her response. She dug it out of her purse, saw Thad's name on the display and debated whether to let it go to voicemail.

"Go ahead and answer it."

If she chose not to, Deb would want an explanation, one Celeste wasn't ready to give. She connected. "Hey, Thad."

Hey, sweetheart."

"How's Zola?" Celeste had met Faith and her little one briefly at the hospital at Faith's insistence.

"She's good. They'll be going home this evening or in the morning. I'm going to visit tomorrow and I'd like for you to come with me. Faith and Brandon are completely okay with it."

Yes, was poised on the tip of her tongue, but she needed to put some distance between them until she knew for sure what she would be facing. "I have a couple of pre-scheduled appointments tomorrow and Wednesday. Maybe I can go another time. Can I call you back? I'm having lunch with Deborah."

"Of course. Tell her I said hello. Honey, is there something bothering you?"

"No, no. I'm fine."

"Are you sure? I'm starting to worry about you."

"Positive. There's no need to worry." He seemed to be able to read her like a book.

"Okay. Just know that I'm here for anything you need."

Celeste closed her eyes briefly as her emotions flared. "I know and I appreciate it."

"I love you, baby."

"I love you, too," she said softly and hung up.

"Usually, when two people are in love, they're excited about spending time together, appointments or not."

"I see the oncologist tomorrow."

"You should have asked him to go with you."

She ran a hand across her forehead. "He doesn't know."

Deborah frowned. "You still haven't told him about the biopsy or anything?"

"No. And I decided that if it's cancer, not to see him again." Although, she had no idea how she would manage that, especially after spending two nights in his arms. She had tossed and turned all last night, wanting to have him next to her.

She let out an exasperated sigh. "Celeste, you have got to be kidding me."

"I can't put him through what I went through with Gary. It was pure torture to watch him suffer that way. You're right. I love Thad and after everything he's had to deal with in the past, I don't want to add to those burdens."

"Thad is a grown man and fully capable of making his own decisions. I can't begin to imagine how hard it was for you those two years, but you can't tell me you would have walked away." Deborah grabbed Celeste's hand. "I know you think you're doing the right thing, but please don't do this, sis. Let him be there for you. I know he'll want to."

Celeste heard everything her sister said, but she remembered those long nights feeling helpless to do anything when Gary's pain had gotten so bad that no amount of medication would work. Thad had lost his wife and daughter, and she wouldn't be able to take it watching him find love, just to lose it again in the blink of an eye. She loved him enough to spare him from all that. Or at least, she hoped she could.

CHAPTER 12

*F*riday morning, Thad sat in the rocking chair with Zola cradled against his shoulder. She seemed to enjoy being snuggled right under his neck and fussed whenever he tried to shift her position.

"You've got her spoiled already, Thad," DeAnna said, coming into the room with Nolan trailing. She kissed the baby on the forehead and Thad on the cheek.

"Hey, what can I say? She loves hanging with her grandpa. "You act like you haven't spoiled Christian, Nyla and Little Omar." Siobhan and her husband, Justin's two-year-old daughter and five-year-old son had Dee wrapped around their fingers. Same with Omar.

She laughed. "I love my grandbabies and I can't wait for Khalil and Lexia's to arrive."

"When is she due again?"

"Mid July." Dee took a seat on the sofa.

"You only have a couple of weeks to wait."

"Unless that one gets impatient like little Miss Zola and comes early," Nolan said.

Dee shook her head. "I don't think so. I talked to Lexia

yesterday and she said she's not having any contractions yet. Where's Celeste? I thought she'd be here."

Pain settled in Thad's chest. He hadn't talked to Celeste since Monday and was at a loss as to why she appeared to backing away from their relationship. "I haven't talked to her all week."

Nolan lifted a brow. "I thought you said everything went well last weekend."

"It did. I don't have a clue what happened between then and now. I asked if something was bothering her a couple of times and she said no." He stopped rocking. "I wish I knew what was going on." Zola squirmed and began to fuss. Thad started rocking again and gently patted her back.

Dee rose from her seat and came to take the baby. "Come on, sweet pea. Let's go find your mommy. Zola and I will leave you two to talk."

Nolan followed Dee's departure, then leaned forward in his chair. "What's going on, Thad?"

Thad let out a frustrated sigh and dragged a hand down his face. "I honestly don't know. I'm in love with Celeste, and it's killing me."

He smiled. "You deserve to have this and I'm glad you've found love again. You mentioned Celeste being a widow. Do you think she's having some guilt?"

"She said she wasn't and that she was ready to move forward with her life. That was before I told her I loved her. Do you think that may have scared her? But she said she loved me, too." The more he thought about it, the more he wondered if he'd moved too fast. Yes, she had reciprocated, but had she meant it or just said it so he wouldn't feel bad. He opened his mouth to share his thoughts and his cell rang. Thad hoped to see Celeste's name on the display, but frowned at the unfamiliar number. "Let me see who this is, Nolan. It could be someone from the mental health center needing to talk." He hit the button. "Hello."

"Thad, it's Deborah, Celeste's sister."

"Hi, Deborah. Is everything okay with TJ?" The young man had called Thad once since that first day at the center and they talked briefly.

"Maybe not fully okay, but he's slowly progressing. But that's not why I called."

"What is it?" he asked with mounting alarm. "Did something happen to Celeste?"

"Not exactly. Lord, she is going to kill me and Emery. But we felt you needed to know that she's having surgery at one o'clock today."

"Surgery?" Thad didn't realize he'd gotten to his feet until he was halfway across the room.

"She's having a breast biopsy."

Thad glanced over at Nolan's concerned gaze and mouthed, "I have to leave. Let Faith and Brandon know and I'll call you when I know something." A minute later, he jumped into his car armed with the hospital information and sped out of the driveway. The surgery wouldn't start for another two hours and he prayed he'd be able to talk to her before then. It took him forty-five minutes to get across town and the drive had tested every inch of his control. He called Deborah as he strode through the parking lot. She told him Emery would meet him in the lobby. He spotted Emery almost immediately after entering the hospital.

"Thank you for coming," Emery said, reaching out to shake Thad's hand. "This way."

"I appreciate the call. How is she?" The two men rounded the corner and took the elevator up to the second floor.

"She's really nervous that they might find cancer."

"How are you holding up? I know this can't be easy for you."

Emery sighed deeply. "I wish I could say I'm okay, but I'm scared to death this is going to be a repeat of what we went through with my father."

Thad placed a hand on Emery's shoulder. "Just know that I'm here if you want to talk."

He stopped and scrutinized Thad. "Do you love my mother?"

"More than my own life," he answered without hesitation.

Seemingly satisfied, Emery continued toward the nurse's station. "This is Thad Whitcomb, my mother's fiancé." He nodded Thad's way. "Mom's probably going to have a fit knowing we called, but she needs you. Even if she doesn't want to admit it." Emery gestured behind them. "She's back there."

Thad kept his surprise hidden at the young man's reference. "And I need her." Thad entered the area and found Celeste talking to Deborah.

Celeste's eyes widened when she noticed him. "*Thad!* What are you doing here?"

"Emery and I decided he needed to be here. Now that he is, I'll be in the waiting room," Deborah said. She gave Thad a grateful smile as she passed and pulled the curtain closed behind her.

Thad moved to Celeste's side, took her hand and kissed her. "Baby, why didn't you tell me? You knew I would've never let you go through this alone. I'd've been right by your side."

Celeste closed her eyes briefly as if trying to gather her thoughts. "I know that. I didn't want you to worry and...if it is cancer—"

"We'll deal with it. Together," he finished.

"I can't ask you to do that. You've been through so much hurt and loss. It nearly killed me to watch Gary suffer and I don't want the same for you."

His heart broke hearing the pain in her voice. The fact that she would sacrifice herself to spare him the same pain made him love her even more. "Sweetheart, I can only imagine how difficult it must have been to see your husband in all that pain and not be able to help. We don't know what the results are going to be, but just like you were there for Gary, I'm going to be here for you. I love you, and this is what love does. We fight side-by-side and survive by any means necessary."

Tears spilled down her face. "I love you so much."

Thad leaned over and grabbed a couple of tissues. He sat on the edge of the bed and gently wiped them away. "This is just like the first day we met."

They shared a smile and Celeste said, "Your words then and now were exactly what I needed."

"From now on, the only tears I want to wipe away are tears of joy. Deal?"

"Deal."

He kissed her to seal the agreement and felt the pressure in his chest ease for the first time since receiving the call. "Deborah and Emery are worried that you're going to be angry with them, but I told them you'd be fine."

Celeste chuckled. "I know they meant well. And they were right this time. I need you in my life, Thad."

"Then that's where I'll be." The nurses and doctor came in to explain more about the procedure and to take her to the operating room. "I'll be here when you open your eyes." The same place he planned to be for the rest of their lives.

CELESTE OPENED THE FRONT DOOR TO LET THAD IN. SHE GAVE him a quick kiss. "I'm almost ready. Be right back."

Thad wrapped an arm around her waist and drew her into his embrace. "What kind of kiss was that? I need a real kiss, not some little peck on the cheek like we're just friends."

Smiling, she pulled his head down, nibbled his bottom lip, teased the corner of his mouth with her tongue, then slid it inside. She slowly and provocatively twirled her tongue around his, eliciting a deep groan from his throat. He quickly took over the kiss, delving deeper into her mouth with a finesse that sent sparks of desire from her head to her toes. At length, she eased back. "How was that?"

"Good, but I want another, you know, just to be sure."

"Later. We're going to be late." She had her post-surgery appointment with the doctor.

Thad swatted her playfully on the butt. "You can't just tease me and leave me hanging."

"It'll give you something to look forward to," Celeste said with a wink as she went to get her shoes and purse. The past two weeks since the surgery had been something out of a dream. Not only had Thad been there when she awakened, but he had also insisted that she stay at his house for the first three days so he could take care of her. During that time, he had treated her like a queen. She never wanted for anything. Even when she'd come back home, he had visited every day after spending time with his granddaughter, cooked for her and continued to care for her every need. He'd even spoken to Celeste's mother. It usually took a lot to impress Rose Blake, but Thad had done it in one five-minute chat. Celeste hadn't been this happy in a long time. She paused in putting on her shoes. She and Gary had a wonderful marriage and now she had been blessed to find even more happiness with Thad. Celeste sent up a quick prayer of thanks, picked up her purse and went back to where Thad sat waiting in the living room. "Okay, thanks for letting me know," she heard him say.

Thad came to his feet and pocketed the phone. "That was Nolan calling to let me know that their fifth grandchild had been born. Khalil and Lexia had a boy."

"That's wonderful news. Emery changes women like he changes his shirt, so I don't think I'll ever get any grandchildren from him."

He chuckled and held her in the circle of his arms. "Then we'll just spoil Zola until he settles down. Ready?"

"Yep. Thanks for going with me."

"Baby, there's no place I'd rather be. I'm so glad everything turned out okay."

"So am I." The surgeon had called a few days ago to let her know that they had removed all the cells and none were malignant. Celeste had been given a new lease on life and she planned to take full advantage.

They drove to the doctor's office and Thad elected to stay in the waiting room when they called her back. The doctor was pleased with the healing process and told her to call if she had any problems.

"What did he say?" Thad asked, rising to his feet when Celeste came back.

She waited until they were in the hallway before answering. "He's happy with how I'm healing and I don't have to come back to see him. I can just get back to my regularly scheduled exams." They exited the building and walked over to his car.

"That's what I like to hear. What are you doing later this evening?" he asked as he started the engine.

"Nothing. Why?"

"I thought we could go out to dinner to celebrate."

"What time?"

"I'll be back to pick you up around six."

"Works for me. All I need to know is if I should be casual or dressy."

"Dressy. We've got to do this celebration right."

Celeste started singing Kool and the Gang's song, "Celebration." Thad joined in and they laughed and sang all the way back to her house. Once there, she took a few minutes to call Deborah and Emery and filled them in on the doctor's report, then she took a long and leisurely bubble bath.

A smile curved her lips when she thought about her and Thad singing in the car. His sense of humor and a playful nature always had a way of making her feel the same freedom she had experienced as a teenager.

Celeste got out of the tub, dried off and dressed. She figured she couldn't go wrong with a little black dress. After fastening the strap of her three-inch heeled sandals, she walked over to the mirror, turning one way, then the other. Her stomach wasn't as flat as she liked and gravity played by its own rules, but she couldn't complain. Thad had told her she'd earned every dip, wrinkle and curve, and he loved them all. Celeste applied her makeup and smoothed down the layered strands of her hair. She briefly speculated on what it might be like to have him with her every night. She missed lying against his chest with his arms wrapped protectively around her as she slept. This wasn't the first time the thought had popped into her head, but they had grown closer over the past couple of weeks and she could see them considering marriage in the future. At least, that's where she hoped they would end up.

She had just spritzed on some of her favorite perfume when she heard the doorbell. She took one last look in the mirror, then headed to the door. "Wow!" That was the only word that came to mind when she saw Thad standing there in a charcoal gray suit that she knew had been tailored expressly for him. "I sure hope I don't have to act up tonight if some woman starts staring at you too long," she teased.

Thad laughed. "I don't think you have to worry about that. Besides, the only woman I want is standing in front of me. I can't even see another woman. Hi, sweetheart." He kissed her lightly, being careful not to smudge her lipstick and escorted her out.

If Celeste didn't already love him, that would have pushed her over the edge. She settled in for the ride. He pulled into his driveway less than half an hour later and she turned her questioning gaze his way.

He got out and came around to her side. "I wanted you all to myself tonight."

She noticed the lit candles first thing when she walked in the door. She sniffed. The fragrant smell of food wafted into her nose. "You cooked?"

"Nope." Amusement danced in his eyes, but he didn't comment further. He led her out to his deck.

Celeste stopped in her tracks. He had transformed the area to resemble a private restaurant. Dim lights had been strung to create a romantic atmosphere and an elegantly set table with long tapers and rose petals had been placed off to one side. "This is... How did you do all this?"

"I had a little help from Dee, Siobhan and Morgan."

The PR director and the sports agent, right?" She remembered the Gray's two daughters from the hospital.

He nodded.

She surveyed her surroundings once more. "I don't know what to say. It's simply beautiful."

Thad pulled out her chair. "Have a seat and I'll be right back."

He came back a minute later with a young woman wearing a chef's jacket and introduced her as Dominique Taylor, a personal chef who owned Dinner by Dominique. She handed them printed menus for the four-course meal she would be serving and teasingly said that she'd leave the dessert course for them to have at their leisure. Celeste scanned the sheet—baby mixed greens with a lemon herb dressing, beef tenderloin crostinis, carmelized salmon with wild rice and sautéed spinach. Her gaze flew to his when she read that they would have chocolate-dipped strawberries. Thad had selected some of her favorite foods. A warm sensation settled between her thighs when she recalled how he'd fed them to her that night at his house and how the evening had ended.

He poured them glasses of wine handed her one and lifted his toward her. "To an evening of love."

She touched her glass to his. "To love." He pressed a few buttons on his phone and music flowed through concealed speakers. As they dined, the heat level rose steadily. Every time she glanced up, she found his eyes waiting. The food had been excellently prepared, but the desire blazing in his eyes, coupled with the sensual jazz and R&B playlist he had created, had her wanting to skip right to dessert. Or after.

"I do believe this is our song." Thad set his napkin aside, came around the table and extended his hand.

Celeste recognized it as the same Brian Culbertson song they had danced to in her kitchen. She placed her hand in his. "I believe you're right." She melted into his arms as they danced. She rested her head on his shoulder and sighed contentedly. She wanted to be with him just this way for the rest of their lives. "I love you, Thad."

"I love you, too. I love you so much, I wish you could see into my soul so you'd know just how deep it goes." He tilted her chin and stared into her eyes. "My everything needs your everything. Your smile, your touch, the feel of your body next to mine—your everything."

She could barely breathe.

"I hope you can hear in my voice and feel in *my* touch that my heart is all in when it comes to you. I not only want to be your friend, but also your partner in life, to have and to hold always and forever. Celeste Williams, will you marry me?" Thad released her and retrieved a small velvet box from his pocket.

Even in the dim lighting, the diamonds caught fire. Celeste thought she might burst from the joy bubbling up and she could only nod. She finally found her voice and whispered, "Yes, I would be honored to be your wife." He slid the ring onto her finger and she launched herself into his arms. Thad kissed her with a passion that let her know that he'd be there to walk beside her no matter what came their way. As he'd said before, love fought side-by-side and survived by any means necessary. Just being with him made her life brighter and she looked forward to all her days being sweeter from now on.

wo months later.

Thad stood next to Nolan at the front of the church waiting for Celeste to make her entrance. Deborah stood across from him, beaming. They had planned to have an intimate gathering, but somehow things had spiraled out of control and nearly every employee of Gray Home Safety had shown up, filling the building to capacity.

"Nervous?" Nolan whispered.

"Not at all. The only reason to be nervous is if you don't know what you're getting." Nolan had said those words to Thad almost forty years ago when their roles were reversed and Nolan stood waiting for DeAnna.

"True that, my brother."

The music started and his breath caught as Celeste came toward him on Emery's arm with s slow sway. Thad caught Celeste's father's gaze and he nodded. Her mother smiled. He'd had an opportunity to talk to them when they arrived two days ago and made the same promise as he had to Emery—that he would always love and protect Celeste. He turned his attention back to the woman who would become his wife in a few short minutes. She had chosen an ivory calf-length dress that hugged every one of her curves and dipped low enough in the front to hint at the sweet treasures he knew were there. When she reached him, it took all he had not to kiss her then and there. Thad heard a low chuckle and shifted to see Brandon's knowing smile. Thad had teased him about kissing Faith before the minister could utter a word and the look on Brandon's face now said he had read Thad's thoughts. He managed to stay in control long enough to recite his vows. When it came time for their first kiss as husband and wife, Thad did his best to let Celeste know this was what she could look forward to from this day forward. He wanted her to feel the depth of his love.

Afterwards, he and Celeste stood waiting for the photographers to set up, talking with Deborah, TJ, Faith and Emery.

Faith hadn't stopped smiling since she walked into the church. "Dad, I am *so* happy for you and Celeste." She grasped Celeste's hands. "I'm looking forward to us getting to know each other even more. Zola is one lucky girl to have a grandmother like you."

"So am I and thank you."

Faith turned to Emery. "I've always wanted a brother. I have to say though, I'm glad I'm the oldest."

They all laughed and Emery said, "Yeah, yeah, but only by a couple of years." He glanced over at Thad. "And your dad is pretty cool."

"Yes, he is."

It pleased Thad to see Faith and Emery getting along. He had assured the young man that he would always be there for his mother and she'd never have a moment of sadness.

"I agree. He's cool," TJ said.

Deborah and Celeste whipped their heads around.

TJ divided his gaze between them. "What? We've talked a few times."

Celeste placed her arm around Thad. "You are such an amazing man."

Thad smiled. The photographer called them over. It took less than thirty minutes to complete the photo shoot, and then he and Celeste slid into the back of the limousine that would take them to the hotel for the reception. "Did I tell you how gorgeous this dress looks on you?"

"You might have mentioned it."

"I am going to enjoy every second of removing it later," he murmured, trailing fleeting kisses along her jaw and neck.

She giggled. "And I can't wait for you to take it off. I also can't wait for you to see what's under it."

His head came up sharply. "You cannot say something like that and expect me to wait hours." He reached for the buttons on the back of the dress.

She scooted away. "What are you doing?"

Thad lifted a brow. "What do you think?"

Celeste laughed. "We are not going to get busy in the back of a limo like a couple of horny teenagers."

"Why not? I promise it'll be fun." He wiggled his eyebrows.

"I'm sure it would be, but we're here." She pointed out the window as the limo drove into the hotel's valet lane.

He groaned.

She patted his cheek. "Don't worry, baby. I'll make it worth the wait, and I won't stop until *you're* satisfied, not until you tell me you've had enough," she said with a sultry smile.

His arousal was swift as he recalled telling her the same thing.

"I promise."

She closed the distance between them and kissed him. Thad rested his forehead against hers. She was his love, his partner in life, his everything. He had finally found his *one* and he would treasure this gift forever.

DEAR READER,

Many of you asked if Thaddeus Whitcomb (introduced in Giving My All To You) would get his own happily-ever-after. I'm pleased to share his and Celeste's journey to love, grown folks style, and I hope you enjoy the ride. There may not be a lot of drama—when you get to a certain age, most times you know what and who you want—but that doesn't mean the road is 100% smooth. However, if they're lucky, forever just may be in the cards. I hope you enjoy this first installment from The Grays Family & Friends series and catching up with the Gray family.

Thank you for your continued encouragement and support. I appreciate you. Remember to drop me a line at sheryllister@gmail.com if you have any questions, comment, or just want to chat. I love hearing from you.

You can also find me:
    Website: www.sheryllister.com
    Facebook: http://www.facebook.com/sheryllisterauthor
    Twitter: @1slynne
    Instagram: sheryllister

Love & Blessings!
    Sheryl

EXCERPT FROM GIVING MY ALL TO
YOU (THE GRAYS OF LOS ANGELES
BOOK 3)

"Hey, girl. You want to do lunch today?"

Faith Alexander smiled. "Sure. I'm just working on one of my web designs." Once or twice a month on a Saturday she and her best friend, Kathi Norris met for lunch. "Hang on, Kathi. Someone's at the door," she said, walking to the front. She opened it and saw the mailman standing there.

He stuck a box into her hands along with a card and pen. "Just sign here, please."

She cradled the phone against her ear, adjusted the box and signed the receipt. "Thank you." Faith closed the door and frowned, not recognizing the sender.

"Helloooo."

Kathi's voice drew Faith out of her thoughts. "Sorry. I just got a box from someone in Los Angeles named Thaddeus Whitcomb."

"Ooh, girl, you've got a man sending you gifts from California?"

"No. I have no idea who this is." She shook the box and heard a slight rustling.

"What's in it?"

"I have no idea," she said, placing it on the desk in the spare bedroom she used as an office.

"Anyway, Cameron—the guy I've been dating—has a cute friend and I thought we could double date," Kathi said.

"No."

"Come on, Faith."

"*No.* The last time I went on one of your little blind double dates it turned into the month from hell. You're on your own this time."

"Grant wasn't that bad."

"Hmph. You weren't the one he was calling ten times a day asking when I was going to let him come to my house. I swear that man had octopus arms and was just as slimy. He made my skin crawl." She shivered with the remembrance.

"Okay, okay, I get your point. He did border on stalking."

"You think?"

"But this guy is different—six feet, rich brown skin, fit and he's easy on the eyes."

"Doesn't matter. I'm not interested." After that fiasco six months ago, she had sworn off men and was content with building her year-old web design business.

"We aren't getting any younger and I'd like to settle down and have a kid or two before my eggs shrivel up and die."

She laughed. "Kathi, you act like we're pushing fifty. We're only thirty." She cut into the box, pulled back the flap and saw a stack of letters with a rubber band around them. All were addressed to her from Thaddeus Whitcomb and had "Return to Sender" written on them. She quickly flipped through them and noted the postmarks went back almost twenty-eight years.

While half listening to Kathi list all the reasons why this guy would be different, Faith opened the gray envelope on the top that had her first name written in large letters and withdrew the sheet of paper. When she unfolded it, a photo of a man wearing an Army uniform and holding a baby fell out. She didn't know who he was, but she recognized the child. She quickly read the letter. Her eyes widened and her heart stopped and started up again. "It can't be. He's supposed to be dead," she whispered in shock. "Kathi, I have to go."

"Wait...what? What about lunch?"

"I need to take a rain check. I'll call you later."

Butterflies fluttered in her belly as she picked up the photo again and studied it for a moment before re-reading the letter. Tears filled her eyes and anger rose within her. She tossed everything back into the box, slid her arms into a light jacket and grabbed the box, her purse and keys and left. Although the sun shone, there was a slight breeze and the early June temperatures in Portland hovered near seventy. Twenty minutes later, she rang her parent's doorbell.

"Faith," her father said with a wide grin, "we didn't know you were coming over. Come in, baby." He kissed her cheek.

"Hi, Dad." Her mother had married William Alexander when Faith was eight and he had been the only father she'd known. "Where's Mom?"

"She's in the family room working on one of those word search puzzles." He placed a hand on her arm as she passed him. "Everything okay, Faith?"

"I don't think so."

His concerned gazed roamed over her face. "Well, let's go talk about it."

Her mother glanced up from her book when they entered and lowered the recliner. "Hey, sweetheart."

"We need to talk, Mom."

Her mother's brows knit together. "Something wrong?"

Faith dropped the box on her mother's lap.

"What is this?"

"You tell me."

Her mother lifted out the envelopes and quickly flipped

through them. Her loud gasp pierced the silence. "Where... where did you get these?"

"They were delivered to my house this afternoon. How could you do this to me, Mom?" She paced back and forth across the plush gray carpet.

"What the heck is going on here?" her father asked. "Who are those letters from?"

She stopped pacing and, not taking her eyes off her mother, Faith answered, "My father. The man she told me died while serving in the Army."

His eyes widened and he dragged a hand down his face. "Francis? Is that true?" he asked.

Her mother tossed the letters aside. "You don't understand," she snapped.

"You're right, I don't." Faith flopped down onto the sofa. "He's been alive all this time and trying to contact me," she murmured, tears gathering in her eyes. "Why, Mom? Why did you lie to me?"

"I was trying to protect you."

"*Protect me?* From what?"

"You were too young to know what it was like when he came home that last time—the crying out, the nightmares with him flailing around the bed, the flashbacks. I was worried he'd hurt you and me, and I didn't want to deal with it every time he came home." She sniffed. "So I left."

Faith couldn't begin to imagine what her father had seen and experienced that would cause such nightmares, but she had a hard time believing that her mom didn't even try to help him. Growing up, she always marveled at her mother's compassionate nature and wanted to grow up to be just like her. Now she was learning that hadn't always been the case. "That still didn't give you the right to just erase him from my life." Faith wiped away her own tears. "And how did you know you would have to deal with it every time?" She paused. "He's invited me to visit him and I'm going."

Her mother jumped up from the chair. "Why? It's been twenty-eight years. What can you possibly gain by going to see him? Just let it be."

"He's my *father* and I'm not going to let it be." She caught her stepfather's gaze. "I'm sorry, Dad. You know I love you." She felt bad because he had always been there for her.

He nodded. "I know, honey. You go do what you have to do. Francis, she has to find her own way."

"Thanks, Dad."

The two women engaged in a stare down for a full minute before her mother turned away. She had never been this angry with her mother. Sure, when Faith was a teen, they'd had their disagreements, but nothing like this.

Her mother pointed a finger Faith's way. "Nothing good can come from this. *Nothing.* I don't know why he's trying to disrupt your life after all these years."

Faith threw up her hands. "Disrupt my life? How is wanting to know your daughter a disruption?" She snatched up the letters. "He's been sending letters for twenty-eight years and you sent them back without ever telling me. The only person who's *disrupted* my life is you." She put the letters in the box and stormed past her mother. "I have to get out of here."

At the door, her stepfather's voice stopped her.

"I know you're pretty angry at your mother right now, but try to see it from her side. She was only doing what she thought best." He gave her a strong hug, palmed her face much like he did when she was a child and placed a gentle kiss on her forehead. "Whatever you decide, I'll always be here." Although approaching his fifty-eighth birthday, he didn't look a day over forty. His walnut colored skin remained unlined, his body was still trim and toned, and his deep brown eyes held the love he had always shown her.

"Thanks, Dad."

"When are you leaving?"

"I don't know."

"Call to let us know you're safe."

"I will." Faith kissed his cheek and slipped out the door.

She drove home still in disbelief over what her mother had done and that her biological father was actually alive. Once there, she called Kathi and filled her in, then searched hotels and reserved a flight and car for the following Tuesday. Although she loved her stepfather, Faith had often imagined what he would be like in person. *Guess I'll find out soon.*

"Are you ready to step into the CEO position, little brother?"

Brandon Gray acknowledged a couple of people leaving the conference room after the Wednesday morning staff meeting ended then smiled at his older sister, Siobhan. "Been ready." His father had started the company more than two decades ago after being discharged from the Army and seeing the difficulties his best friend, who had been wounded in combat, had trying to get services and accommodations. Instead of waiting around, Nolan Gray began designing them himself. What started in their home garage had now grown to be one of the largest in-home safety companies in the country. Their father would step down at the end of the month, leaving Brandon as head of Gray Home Safety. His father's best friend, Thaddeus Whitcomb, who they affectionately called Uncle Thad, joined the company shortly after it was formed and served as the company's vice president. He planned to retire, as well. The two men had always said that the reins would be turned over to their children, with a Gray in the CEO position and a Whitcomb as Vice President.

Siobhan stuffed some papers into a folder. "I wonder what Uncle Thad is going to do. Too bad he never got married or had kids. And as good-looking as he is, I'm surprised. I don't ever remember seeing him date."

"I saw one woman coming around for a while when I was working in the warehouse that summer after junior year in high school, but I don't know what happened to her."

"Well, with no one to step in at vice president, you'll be in charge of everything."

"True." Brandon actually preferred it that way, expected it after all this time. While the roles worked well for his dad and uncle, he'd much rather work solo.

Their father came around the table. "Brandon, can you come by my office? I need to talk to you."

Brandon studied his father's serious expression. "Sure, Dad. I'll be right there."

His father clapped him on the shoulder and exited.

Siobhan said, "I wonder what that's about."

He shrugged. "I don't know."

"Well, let me know what happens."

"Okay." Brandon left the room and started down the corridor leading to his father's office. He spoke to the administrative assistant, who told him to go in.

"I just hope this time you can get the answers," he heard his father say.

"Dad? Oh, hey Unc. I didn't know you were here."

"Hi, Brandon. I'll talk to you later, Nolan." The two older men shared a glance that wasn't lost on Brandon.

He followed his uncle's departure. Today he was on crutches. He'd lost the lower part of his left leg during Desert Storm and typically used a prosthetic. However, over the past year, Uncle Thad had taken to using his wheelchair or the crutches because of problems with the artificial limb.

After Uncle Thad left, Brandon's father said, "Close the door and have a seat, son."

He complied. "What's going on, Dad?"

"There may be a little delay in you taking my position."

"What? Why?"

"Something has come up that needs to be handled before we pass on the reins."

"If you tell me what it is, maybe I can help."

"No, no," his father answered quickly. "I'll handle it."

He tried to keep his surprise and distress hidden. Brandon knew he could be intense sometimes, but he was the best person for the job. He knew this company inside out. "How long are you talking?"

"I'm not sure. Another month or two perhaps."

He did his best to remain in his seat and not behave like the hotheaded teen he used to be. Was his father having second thoughts about Brandon heading the company? He was afraid to ask, but needed to know. Taking a deep, calming breath, he asked, "Are you thinking of putting someone else in the position."

"No."

Something—he didn't know what—in his father's tone gave Brandon pause. "Is that all?"

"Yes." His father released a deep sigh. "Son, I know you're upset, but I assure you this is just temporary."

Brandon stood and nodded. "Since it's almost five, I'm going to take off, unless you need me to stay."

He shook his head.

"Tell Mom hi."

"I will."

He stalked back to his desk, locked up and set out for the gym his brother, Khalil, owned. The former model was now a highly sought after personal trainer. With rush-hour traffic, it took Brandon nearly an hour to reach his destination, which incensed him even more. He was more than ready to take out his frustrations on the heavy bag.

"Damn, big brother. You might want to go easy on that bag."

Ignoring Khalil for the moment, Brandon continued with his punches. A few minutes later, winded, he removed his gloves, wiped his face with a towel and downed a bottle of water.

"Want to tell me what's going on and why you're about to dislodge my bag from the ceiling?"

He took up a position next to Khalil on the wall. "Dad is postponing his retirement. He said something came up that he needs to handle and it could be another couple of months."

"Why can't you handle it?"

"I offered, but he wouldn't even tell me what it was. It's bugging the hell out of me. I'm almost positive Uncle Thad is in on it, too." Brandon recalled the shared look between the two men.

Khalil swung his head in Brandon's direction. "I know he's not thinking about putting someone else in the CEO position. Granted, you do go over the top sometimes, like when that couple was trying to sue the company last year. You're lucky Siobhan and Morgan are still speaking to you."

He shot his brother a dark glare. "Shut up." When the accusations were first leveled, Siobhan, the company's PR director, had been out of town with her now husband and missed several calls that weekend. Their baby sister, Morgan, had been tasked to handle the legal case and, unbeknownst to the family, had become agent to a star football player. Both times, Brandon had confronted his sisters, feeling that they should have put the company first. Needless to say, it hadn't won him any brownie points. While Siobhan still worked for the company, Morgan had left the company six months ago and was doing well in the world of sports management. She had also married said football player. "Dad said he wasn't looking to place anyone else in the position, but I have a bad feeling about this."

"Thank God, because I'm certainly not going to do it, and neither is Malcolm." Their youngest brother, Morgan's twin, played professional football and had no interest in doing anything not sports related. Khalil straightened from the wall. "Well, you've waited all this time for the position. Another few weeks won't kill you." Brandon grunted and Khalil laughed. "Besides, it'll give you more time to practice some patience."

Brandon grabbed his stuff and left Khalil standing there. He spent another forty-five minutes lifting weights before calling it a night. To add to his already foul mood, he realized that he'd forgotten to add a change of clothes and, after showering, had to put his wrinkled slacks and dress shirt back on. He spotted Khalil on his way out working with a client and threw up a wave.

At his car, Brandon tossed his gym bag in the back seat then climbed in on the driver's side, started the engine and drove off. His stomach growled, letting him know it was far past the time for him to eat. As he merged onto the freeway, his cell rang and he engaged the Bluetooth device. "Hello."

"Brandon, can you stop by Thad's and pick up a folder for the meeting tomorrow morning?"

"Hey, Dad. I thought he was going to be there."

"He planned to, but the orthopedic clinic had a cancellation and can see him sooner than his original appointment two months from now."

Brandon knew how difficult it was to get an appointment with a specialist and understood the necessity of taking anything that came along earlier.

"I'd go, but your mother and I are on our way out and won't be back until late."

"I'll take care of it."

"Thanks. I'll see you in the morning."

Groaning, Brandon reversed his course and headed in the opposite direction. Twenty minutes later, he parked behind Uncle Thad's black Buick, got out and started up the walkway. Unlike the other houses on the block, this one had no steps leading to the door, which made it easier for him to maneuver his crutches or wheelchair. He rang the bell and, while waiting, scanned the meticulously groomed yard. Brandon remembered mowing it on many weekends growing up. The grass had turned brown in spots, but that was to be expected with the drought.

"Brandon, come on in."

He turned at the sound of his uncle's voice and stepped inside. "Hey, Unc. I see you still keep the yard looking good."

Uncle Thad smiled. "You know I wouldn't have it any other way." He adjusted his crutches and led the way further into the house. "Sorry you had to go out of your way. I know you probably have things to do so I won't keep you." The inside of the house was just as neat, with not a speck of dust to be found anywhere, despite his bachelorhood. He picked up a manila folder from the dining room table and handed it over.

"Thanks. Dad or I will fill you in when you get back." Brandon retraced his steps to the front door.

"All right. See you Friday."

He loped down the walk to his car, got in and backed out of the driveway. His stomach growled again. He had a steak marinating that he planned to grill and pair it with some potatoes and an ear of corn, but he was so hungry he didn't think he'd last the time it took to prepare the meal. But he didn't want to stop for fast food, either. The good thing was that Unc's house wasn't far from the freeway. He shifted his gaze from the road briefly to check the dash clock. Seven-thirty. Hopefully, at this hour, he would have missed a good portion of the traffic. Brandon eased onto the highway and immediately saw that it was still a little heavy, but not too bad. His cell rang again. He sighed and connected.

"You were supposed to stop by my office and tell me what Dad wanted," Siobhan said as soon Brandon answered. "I went to your office and your assistant said that you left before five. You *never* leave before five. What happened?"

He sighed, not really wanting to talk about it. "I just thought I'd leave a little early today, Vonnie, that's all."

"Mmm hmm, and you didn't answer my question."

Rather than risk his sister coming to his house tonight—and she definitely would to get answers—Brandon gave in. "He's postponing his retirement." He repeated what he'd told Khalil.

"That's strange. Well, at least you'll still get the position."

"Yeah, but—" A truck cut across the highway and hit something in the road that flew through the windshield of a car in the next lane a few lengths ahead. The car swerved and crashed into the center divide. Brandon let out a curse, flipped on his hazard lights and eased to a stop in front of the car. "There's an accident. I'll call you back."

Luckily, the shoulder was wide enough for the crashed car to be out of oncoming traffic. He jumped out, cell phone in hand and, being careful to stay closer to the shoulder, sprinted back to the passenger side of the car while dialing 911. He peered through the window and saw a woman inside. He gave the dispatcher the location and told him that the woman was conscious, but that a pipe of some sort was imbedded in her right shoulder. Brandon couldn't tell whether it had gone in deep or if it was just the deployed airbag holding it in place. "Miss, are you okay?" he called through the slightly open window.

She moaned, tried to push the airbag out of her face with her left hand and rolled her head in his direction. Her eyes fluttered closed and opened again.

In the fading sunlight, Brandon could see bits of glass in her hair and blood on her cheek where she had been cut. "Can you unlock the doors?" For a moment he thought she had passed out, then he heard the click of the lock. He opened the door and, being careful of all the glass on the seat, leaned in. "Help is on the way. What's your name?"

"Faith," she whispered.

"Faith, I'm Brandon. Are you hurt anywhere else besides your shoulder?"

"I…I don't know. Every…thing…hurts." Her eyes closed again.

"Faith, I need you to stay with me." He backed out and started to go around to the driver's side.

She moaned again. "Please…please don't leave."

"I'm just coming around to your side." He waited for a break in the traffic and hurried around to the driver's side. Once there, he carefully opened the door and managed to give her some breathing room from the airbag. Brandon reached for her hand, his concern mounting. "Are you still with me?" She muttered something that sounded like yes. Brandon was momentarily distracted when another person approached.

"Is she okay, man? I called 911."

"Thanks. She's hanging in there." It seemed like an eternity passed before he heard the sirens. *Finally.*

When the paramedics and police arrived, Brandon stepped back. A police officer called him over to give a statement and his gaze kept straying to where the medical team was getting her out of the car and onto a gurney. Faith cried out and it took everything in him not to rush over. He finished his account and stood by watching with the other two people who had eventually stopped.

"Is one of you named Brandon?" a paramedic called out.

Brandon strode over. "Yeah. Me."

"She's asking for you."

He smiled down at her strapped down on the gurney. In the fading sunlight, he could see her face starting to swell where the airbag had hit her. "You're in good hands now."

"Thank you," Faith said, her voice barely audible. "My stuff…my…"

He took it to mean she wanted her things from the car. "I'll get them." To the paramedic he asked, "What hospital are you taking her to?" After getting the information, he walked back and retrieved her purse, keys and a small bag from the back seat. Why was he thinking about going to the hospital? He'd done his civic duty. It would be easy to hand off her belongings to one of the officers and be on his way. But for some reason, he needed to make sure—for himself—that she was okay. Brandon slid behind the wheel of his car and, instead of going home, merged back onto the freeway and headed to the hospital.

DISCOVER SHERYL LISTER

Harlequin Kimani
Just To Be With You
All Of Me
It's Only You
Be Mine For Christmas (Unwrapping The Holidays Anthology)
Tender Kisses (The Grays of Los Angeles Book 1)
Places In My Heart (The Grays of Los Angeles Book 2)
Giving My All To You (The Grays of Los Angeles Book 3)
A Touch Of Love
Still Loving You

Other Titles
Made To Love You
It's You That I Need
Perfect Chemistry
Embracing Forever (Once Upon A Bridesmaid Book 3)
Love's Serenade (Decades: A Journey Of African American Romance Book 3)

ABOUT THE AUTHOR

Sheryl Lister is a multi-award winning author who has enjoyed reading and writing for as long as she can remember. After putting writing on the back burner for several years, she became serious about her craft in 2009. When she's not reading or writing, Sheryl can be found on a date with her husband or in the kitchen creating appetizers and bite-sized desserts. Sheryl resides in California and is a wife, mother of three and former pediatric occupational therapist. She is a member of RWA, CIMRWA, the Kiss of Death Chapter of RWA, and is represented by Sarah E. Younger of Nancy Yost Literary Agency.

facebook.com/sheryl.lister.5

twitter.com/1Slynne

46938325R00083

Made in the USA
Columbia, SC
27 December 2018